KRISTO

By Andrew Datsiouk

Order this book online at www.trafford.com
or email orders@trafford.com

Most Trafford titles are also available at major online book retailers.

Edited by Roma Datsiouk and Gaby Molpeceres

Printed in the United States of America.

ISBN: 978-1-4269-5083-4 (sc)
ISBN: 978-1-4269-5082-7 (e)

Trafford rev. 12/29/2010

North America & international
toll-free: 1 888 232 4444 (USA & Canada)
phone: 250 383 6864 ✦ fax: 812 355 4082

Dear reader,

Imagine yourself a wonderful place on earth, that was gifted by its' nature every thing most beautiful and picturesque, where everything lived, sang, bloomed, where you could observe the most gorgeous birds and animals, where blossomed the prettiest flowers, where the trees were covered in the thickest foliage. The grass here was the greenest and juiciest and it covered the near hills and valleys, on which herded all kinds of animals. During the summer time, the sun was almost always shinning, making this place even more colourful. The rain too would not forget to join in leaving on his path sparkly little drops on the leaves and filling every hollow where any animal could satisfy its' thirst with the purest water.

We can certainly not forget about spring time, which would arrive earlier than usually, unlike on other places on earth. All of a sudden everything would come alive. Since there are many little hills, the melting of the snow created many little creeks which carried its' waters through the valleys in its' crust of ice that reflected the golden sun rays.

Unlike spring, the golden autumn would arrive a bit later. Probably because summer did not want to leave this place and its' little and bigger friends, its' singing, jumping, crawling creatures. But nothing could be done, you had to make way for the next season. Especially in autumn many of them stored up food for the winter. The sweet and wild fruits, juiciest grass, with the mix of different kinds of nuts you could find in any lair and hollow. Believe it or not but not even the smallest bird ever left its' nest and even more surprisingly even more birds would migrate from far away and settle in their old places left untouched after their departure during fall. Usually they nested along the shores of two not very big but very beautiful lakes that would never freeze during winter.

Winter as well left something behind that brought happiness to every living in this place. It was not cold. The snow laying on the ground was always soft and fluffy. If you think that at this time of the year every thing was sleepy and hidden, I would tell you that you are wrong. Of coarse at this time of the year there are cloudy days, and only then will you rarely see someone in the daytime. Though when the sun would come out then you could observe many different groups of animals which came out of their lairs and played all kinds of games. Here and there you could see families of deers and moose coming out of the woods and groves to toss the snow and grab a bite of last year's grass. You could always hear the beautiful singing of a little bird which was heard from a tree not far away.

Every thing lived, sang, and rejoiced there.

I am not going to tell you who exactly lived and sang there. You know them already, and probably even met them.

And to all of these amazing things I have something to add. In the middle of all of this beauty, right in the center, raised a lonely mount. Like every thing else surrounding it, it reflected the prettiest colours. It was almost completely covered in thick vegetation and only the top was covered by a layer of the purest light blue snow that glared under the sun brighter than a giant diamond.

Like elsewhere, the mount was inhabited by different kinds of birds and animals. You could see bears, lynx, cougars. Eagles were hovering around. At night you could hear the owls. They lived every where.

At the bottom of the mountain lived a weird bird. No one new who she was and where she came from. Every one that encountered her could not resist laughing at her. Somebody said that she flew from a very hot country probably because she took the wrong course. Whether it is true or not, no one knows. Nevertheless, she lived alone and never bothered anyone. She was probably shy because of her odd looks.

I will come back to her later on.

And now I have to reveal the secret about this mount no one knew for 300 years.

The thing is that not far from that place where this weird bird lived was a cave. You could hardly see it because it was hidden by a big spiky dark-green bush on which grew blue fruits similar to pears though very bitter. The entrance didn't seem too big and that is why only someone of the size of an average dog could get in. As you entered the cave you would find yourself in a very big room. There was barely any light. It is only during the daytime that single ray of sunlight would penetrate through and lightly brighten up the gloomy place with damp dark-grey walls. For many many years no one dared to go inside. The horrific legends of this cave was scaring everybody wandering around away from it. As if behind the cave deep under the mountain live scary creatures with burning tails, big teeth, and long claws. But let's go back inside. And if you let your eyes get used to the gloomy light, then at the very end you could see another entrance blocked half-way by stones in which there was just enough room to get through. Right after you find yourself in front of a long and narrow corridor. The ceilings were as low so it was hard to move around. You could hear the echoes of strange sounds bouncing against the walls of the cave that could be heard outside. But since everybody that lived on and around the mountain lived in peace, they got used to those sounds and did not pay any attention to them. Legends were left as legends, and the sounds coming out of it were considered as the ones of a scared bat flying inside the cave. Nevertheless, we will go beyond and as we will find out, deep down inside, life really exists. For that we need to go down the long corridor for about three hours. The further you go, the louder the strange sounds become giving you goose bumps. Fortunately, they were not heard as often giving the time to relax a bit and move on.

And now imagine yourself, that after the frightening adventure through this dreadful tunnel coming to its' end, was an even fearful panorama. Imagine it to yourself and you won't be wrong. It is exactly what appears before your eyes. Entering in… I would even say stepping through something and perhaps you begin thinking that you are in another dimension. No. It is exactly that place that appears in front of you. Imagine you are looking beyond and are trying to see the end of something, but you can not. In any direction you would look, you would not see the end of it. That is how big this place was. In front of you was a big stone valley. And only by looking up you could see the end of something. You would probably ask yourself; why is it still possible to distinguish something? It is because at the bottom of the valley, lived horribly looking creatures walking back and forth. At that moment, when someone opened their eyes, a flash of light would appear in the darkness. There was thousands of them. Though they were not all doing it simultaneously and that is why semi-darkness reigned. Would you like to know what they looked like? Ok. They were four-legged monsters with a pair of hands ending with two long claws up to six inches long. The head was surprisingly small on which two twenty inch ears grew with the back covered in scales. Instead of noses, they had a hose that we would probably call a small trunk. Their upper body was also covered in scales under which grew rough, thick, long, fur almost reaching the ground. What was the most frightful thing was their teeth with their two huge fangs. They could easily crack a ten pound stone in two pieces without feeling any pain. I have already talked about their eyes. They were brightening up the way in which they were moving (though they were moving meaninglessly) and at the same time lightening up the valley. They did not have any tails.

But let's leave them behind for a little while because seeing them gives you shivers. Let's rather go further and we will see that the adventure will bring us to an underground river which was not too deep in some places, maybe just two feet deep. In width, the river was not more than twenty feet. The water was very cold but it was crystal clear. You will not believe, but if you get close to the shore or get on a rock sticking out of the water, and closely look at the bottom, then you can observe shiny little stones of all sorts of colours. You guessed it. They were rubies, sapphires, emeralds, and other precious stones. That was the kind of river it was! But let's cross this river and go even further. Approximately in a mile, we will reach a stone wall. If you think that is the end of our adventure, you are wrong. A couple of yards to the right you could easily distinguish an entrance through which penetrated a bit of light. You would probably think that it is an exit from the valley to the outside, but you will be wrong. It was an opening to another world. Gather your patience and lets enter that world. It appears that it turns into a corridor that is just ten feet long. And it is without too much difficulties that we got through. Coming out of it opens a different picture, unlike the one you have seen on the other side. There was a lot of light here. The air was very clean and even the stone walls behind us did not seem as grey. It was also a big open space which you could not determine the end of. If you look beyond, you can observe a narrow, silver, winding stream. It was the same river we have seen before on our path. Somewhere beneath the mountain, it was changing directions and ended up where we are currently standing. Along the river you could see little green isles.
We do not know yet what they represented but we will soon.

And now what could really surprise you, and the reason why you would widely open your eyes and mouth and be unable to say a word, is a noise. A noise that was made by someone. Who would that be? You would ask. I have an answer. There were creatures that looked a lot like our dogs that lived in this place. This noise was made by the young generation that inhabited that place. Split in groups, they were playing some kind of games. You could then hear cheerful shouts and laughs coming from afar. I will now describe them. In size, they were not bigger than our fox-terriers. Everyone of them was exclusively as black as coal. The fur was short but soft. Only at the end of their paws was there a lot of it. It looked like they were wearing fur boots in the middle of the summer. Their muzzles looked a bit like those of a schnauzer without the long beard and eye-brows. They had a large muscle chest. The body was held by slim and strong legs. The eyes were small and round and were also very black. But they had two peculiarities which differentiated them from our little brothers. First - were their ears. You would not believe… but one of the ears was in a triangular shape but the other one was round which gave their muzzles a bit of an unusually funny look. But after spending a bit of time with them, you happen not to notice it anymore. Though you could easily see their other peculiarity. I would even say even more, you have to notice it and be very careful when near it. It was a tail. Unusual. About fifteen inches long ending with a little brush which lit up throughout the day and it was a good idea not to touch it because you could burn yourself. It is why there was so much light in that place. Imagine yourself when everybody comes out of their houses in the morning and thousands of tails/light-bulbs light up. It becomes as bright as day on the mountain we descended. But when everybody went to sleep and tucked their tails under them, only then it became dark.

How they got there you would ask? Gather your patience. In not too long you will find out.

But for now let's go back to those creatures. It turns out it was not just any place where some lived. It was tiny but it was a country. And it was named Kretonia. The name of every Kretonian started with a "K". Interesting is in it? I'm sure you have never heard of anything like it. Kretonians were very smart and were well raised. If you would wander down their streets, you would see schools and daycares where they got their education.

You would ask, what schools? What daycares? Somewhere under a mountain. Do not be surprised, it is the truth. I was amazed myself but that is how it is. Just imagine, you are walking down the street, and on one side lays a huge rock on which you can read "School". Around this rock, walls were build in the shape of a square so that during class time no one from outside could interrupt. Looking inside you could see the student's desks. They were simply flat and well-polished rocks. It was a stony country. In the very middle was installed a plate made of black granite big enough so you could write on it. They wrote with ordinary chalk just like us extracting it not far from their habitat. The main subjects were history where they learned their past, mathematics, and botany. Kretonians had a surprisingly well developed memory because everything the teacher said and explained had to be memorized. They did not have any notebooks.

Adults kept themselves busy as well. Remember those green isle we saw along the shore a while back? They were small gardens where Kretonians grew vegetables and herbs. They also grew (bread) which they grinded into flour.

They never had any shortages of food as well as water thanks to the river.

Next to the wheat field, there were section where Kretonians grew cotton. Which after the harvest proceeded into small factories. In the factories worked skilled and mature female Kretonians. From where you could heard old Kretonian songs.

The male population was occupied with some harder labour. They gathered the wheat, grinded it, after which they poured the grains into bags made out of that same cotton. After every full load, the bag was delivered to the mill on the shoulder. At the mill were grinders that transformed the grains into flour. The work of a grinder was the hardest because they did not have any grind stones like we do so they had to crush the grains with the use of a pestle which were poured into a hollow stone. Every thirty minutes they had to switch place because the work was so hard. After work, very tired though very happy, all together went to the river for a swim to relieve their fatigue.

You can ask yourself, how can all this grow under a mountain where there is nothing but stone and everything we see is so unreal. But this is real.

Having spent some time there, I do not doubt that nature could have created such a wonder. Maybe mother nature knew and prepared this place in advance knowing someone would be living there.

That is why among rocks, the soil happened to be so fertile and everything mentioned before grew. The river also helped, on the shores of which grew short bushes. Throughout the years, Kretonians have learned to treat them and plant them out in different places. By always trimming it, they realized that the bush turned into a tree which they could use to build something.

We cannot help mentioning that in certain underground places in Kretonia, clay was extracted from which they made dishes.

As we can see, it was a diligent population.

I would also like to mention that Kretonians are very peaceful. During all the time that I have spent there, I have not seen anyone in a quarrel. Everybody was very polite. It is with a lot of respect that the old generation lived, which like everybody else made noise by discussing the latest news.

I think time has come now to get closer to Kretonians and get to know them a bit better.

Let's take a look in one of the houses which was not too far from the river. Inside we will see that it is one big room approximately twenty feet long and ten feet wide. In three corners of the room were three beds, two small ones and a bigger one. There was a thick layer of straw on top of the beds which they brought from the fields. They stocked up on straw after the harvest. On top of the straw laid a blanket made by the weavers. The favourite place was the dining room where they all gathered together to eat and discuss the latest new. The family consisted of four Kretonians.

As the supper was over, the mother cleaned up the table. Her name was Kvila and her daughter Kerta was helping her out. Kerta was young and still attended the daycare and was very curious. She showered her mother with questions, who did not always have the answers. That is when the father would come in to help. The parents were very happy to see their daughter growing to be very curious but sometimes they looked at each other wondering what is going to happen when Kerta would start going to school since her outlook on life is growing, wanting to know more, and wanting an answer to each of her questions. There is nothing that could be done said the father, we have to be patient and share all our knowledge with her.

The mother worked at the bakery for fifteen years now. Other female Kretonians working with her had a lot of respect for her and decided one day to make her the head of the bakery. Like nobody else, she brought a great working atmosphere. If there was someone who would start a coral, that would be her. But she also knew how to get the work done.

The father worked in one of the school teaching mathematics and botany and was also very well respected among students and colleagues. During his free time, occupied himself in the cultivation of different kinds of plants and flowers. If you take a look in his small backyard, you can see how many pots there are from which grew distinct plants that we have never seen before. It was him who created few sorts of flowers which then decorated the entrances of many houses in Kretonia.

It is now time to introduce you to the older brother of this family. His name is Kristo. He has graduated from school a while ago and has been working at mill for some time now. His job consisted of carrying the full bags of flour to specific place where they were stored. The distance from the mill to the storage place was about a hundred yards long. It is why this job demanded strong and endurable young males as was Kristo. You could even notice how he differentiated from the others. Kristo was very physically developed. His muscular body was very noticeable under his fur. When he was walking back home, you could see how young females looked at him, then whispered something, and sighed watching him walk by. His intellectuality was at the highest level. He perfectly knew botany and mathematics. But his favourite subject was history. Father always asked him:

"Kristo, why would you not work as a teacher?

"I do not think that I am ready yet. I want to know even more.

Very often his friends would see him pensive, but tried not to disturb his thoughts. But it does not mean that he was an anchorite. When he had the chance, Kristo always joined a group of Kretonians alike, and headed to the river to play games or measure their strength.

And one of those days, after well resting on the shore of the river, and having supper with his family, Kristo decided to share his thoughts with his father. He waited until his father would head to the garden as usually, and so he followed him.

"Father, I would like to speak with you."

"Yes, I am listening, and I think it is time for us to have a talk. I noticed that there is something that has been bothering you for quite some time now. Tell me what it is."
He sat next to him and got ready to listen.

"Father, for a very long time I have been tormented by a question: "I wonder if another life exists outside of ours?" I have a hard time believing that we and the creatures leaving on the other side are the only ones. During all my studies, no one has ever given their thoughts on this subject, not the students nor the teachers. But something is telling me that there is another world somewhere. I will try to explain to you my remarks. I noticed that approximately six months a year, under the arc of our mountain, at a certain time bares all sort of small creeks which flow down to our river. It is the first thing to which I would like to get an answer to."

Secondly:

"Father, during the year you often go to the river. Have you not noticed that during those few months, the water becomes warmer than usually? One more thing, though it is something I have always kept a secret, I will now tell you."

"Around the same time last year, when the water got warmer, I joined my friends to go to the river as usually after work. Somehow it happened during a game that Kliko - my friend, missing the target threw the rock almost in the middle. Since I was the closest one standing, I had to go and get it myself. Jumping from rock to rock, I got to that place. When

9

I was about to take it out of the water, I saw something that I have never seen before. I do not even know what to call it. It was very small. It was in this kind of shape. And Kristo grabbed a rock in the shape of an oval. It had two eyes in the front and what I thought was a mouth in the middle because it kept opening and closing after which appeared tiny bubbles on the surface of the water. From the top, bottom, and the sides, it looked something like fans. They were always in movement as if someone was blowing on them. And then I decided to touch it. But as soon as I put my paw in the water, it twitched and disappeared under water. After that incident, I kept going back to the same place after work for a long time, but have not seen it since. It is why I think that the river does not only flow under the mountain but also brings its' waters elsewhere. These are the mysteries that bother me."

"And now tell me father, what you think of all this?"

"Hmmm..." first thing the father pronounced. But after a long pause he said

"You know Kristo, I am very pleased to see that you happen to be so intrusive, these questions are very mysterious indeed, and I too would like to get some answers to them. But it is hard for me because I do not know myself why all this is happening and where that creature in the water appeared from. I have an advice for you though."

"Have you ever heard of the old Kroople who lives at the very end of our country?"
"No, why?"

"It is said that in the middle of our population there are rumours that he knows many different legends about us and told many stories in which no one wanted to believe in. I have never heard them, that is why I can not say anything. This is why I am thinking of sending you to him so you find out for yourself. I am afraid you will have a hard time making him talk. Someone told me a few years ago that the old Kroople has stopped communicating with us; apparently because no one wanted to believe him."
"But why?" asked Kristo.

"Listen son, we have been living under this mountain for a hundreds of years now. And as you see, we are living very well. Kretonians are used to everything and think that is the way. They are used to the fact that only this mountain, this river, and this life exists. This is why they did not want to listen to the old one."

"But if you really want to, then go see him. Maybe you will be lucky. He lives not far from the place where we extract our granite. Do you know where that is?"

"I do know," said Kristo.

"Then good luck to you son."

Thanking his father, Kristo went back in the house, laid down on his bed and closed his eyes. He was not sleeping, but thinking about the old Kroople. During this time, Kerta ran up to him a few times to see if he was actually sleeping or just laying there. She wanted to play some game with him. The mother noticed it and asked her not to bother her brother.

"Sweet heart! Kristo is very tired from work and that is why he went to bed a bit earlier than usually. Instead, come help me clean out the table in the dining room."

Soon after came back the father and everybody started to get ready for bed. An hour later, they all slept tight, except for Kristo. He was now laying with his eyes open and continued his thinking. He was happy that he opened up to his father and in return did not try to change his mind but instead gave him a good advice. After that conversation, Kristo got even more excited about the idea of another world. He became certain that the old Kroople could help him solve his mystery. After a long reflection, he decided that the first day off, he would go to the old Kroople. After which he fell asleep.

First thing in the morning, Kristo calculated when will be his first day off. It happened to be in four days. That is in a while he thought. But you he had to be patient. So that time goes by faster, Kristo occupied himself with anything he could find just so that day would come as fast as possible.

The day finally came.

Waking up a bit later as usually, he joined his family at the table for breakfast.

Mother had finished putting food in the plates, just in time. Everybody had a fresh piece of bread with a warm herbal drink.

Finishing his breakfast, Kristo thanked his mother, kissed Kerta on the nose, and proceeded to the door.

"Where are you going?" asked mother. "Usually you are home until noon."
"I need to meet up with Kliko. We need to discuss the birthday present we will give to our friend Korry."
"Please, wish him a happy birthday for me if I happen not to see him." asked mother.
"Of course," said Kristo. "Thank you."

As he headed towards the exit.

Walking by his father, he slowed down and simply looked at him.

His father knew.

"Good luck," he said in a low voice, because it was their little secret.

Kerk (was the name of Kristo's father) was not worrying much about the meeting between his son and the old Kroople. There was something that got to him and bothered him after the conversation he had with Kristo. It is alright, thought Kerk. He is still young. It is that age. Everything will be alright.

About an hour later, Kristo finally got to the place which his father told him about. But since he did not know the exact address, he had to ask some Kretonian that was passing by.

"Could please tell me if you know an old Kroople that lives somewhere around this place?"

"Yes I do know," said the stranger with a surprised look on his face

"You need to walk another hundred meters up the street, and on your left you will see the last house. That is where he lives."

"Thank you very much," said Kristo as he started to walk towards the indicated path.

The closer he got the more anxious he got. Finally getting to the house, Kristo stopped and took a deep breath. After standing there for a while, he got back to normal. He then knocked at the door with a stone that was hanging on a rope next to the door. But no one answered. A few seconds later, he knocked again.

"Who is there?" a voice said coming from behind the door.

"My name is Kristo and I would like to meet with grand-father Kroople, is that you?"

"Perhaps," said a trembling but confident voice.

"What do you want Kristo? Where do you come from?"

"I live in a village three kilometres south from here. My father's name is Kerg, he teaches mathematics and botany in the local school. My mother's name is Kvila, she is the head of the bakery."

"Grand-father Kroople, I came to you to discuss something. I have questions to which the answers only you know according to my father."

"What else did your father tell you?"

"He said that you know a lot of stories about our society."

"Your father was wrong. I do not know any stories. So go away. I am sick and do not want to see anyone."

As Kristo heard the sound of leaving steps.

He tried to knock again, this time more quietly. But the answer was unheard.

Very upset, Kristo turned around and headed home. Coming back, he got to the river and decided to sit for a while and take a moment to think of what to do next. The calmness of the river help him calm down a little. I need to meet with the old one anyway, he said to himself. I will go there as many times as needed. And he will let me in.

Kristo did not even notice as he was talking to himself, that Kliko and Korry joined him.

"Hey Kristo! Who are you talking to? No one is around," said Kliko with a smile.

"I think our friend met a ghost and is having a soulful conversation," said Korry laughing.

"Of course not, what are you talking about?" said Kristo embarrassed. "I am just sitting here."

"Oh I know! You are probably writing a poem again," said Kliko.

"You guessed it my friend," said Kristo with a smile trying to avoid needless questions. And just to prevent other ones he asked them himself:

"And what are you two doing here?"

"We came for a dip," said Korry. "Would you like to join us?"

"With pleasure!"

And all three jumped in the water splashing each other and laughing loudly. After resting on the shore, they started playing their favourite game, the game of stones.

That is how the second half of the day passed by helping Kristo getting his good mood back.

He came back home right in time for supper. Mother was already setting up the plates on the table.

"Ah, here is my son!" she said. "You are probably very hungry since you missed lunch."

"Very," admitted Kristo. "May I have two servings?"

"Of course!" said mother.

Soon after, Kerg and Kerta joined in. Being the first one to finish, thanking his mother as always, he went to the backyard knowing his father would soon come. That is how it happened.

"So?" with a quiet but interested voice asked Kerg.

"Nothing for now," said Kristo.

"Did you see him?"

"No."

"Talked?"

"Just a little through the door."

"What did you ask him?"

-"I asked him to see me, but he said he did not want to see anyone and told me to leave."

Kerg sighed and after a short pause asked:
"What will you do?"

Kristo confidently looked at his father and said:
"I will go back."
"What if he does not let you in again?"
"I will keep going back until he does."
"I agree, do not give up son."

Kerg was proud of his son. He knew that he would achieve his goal and simply asked:
"When will you go back?"
"Next week, on my next day off."

Kristo was standing in front of the familiar house with full of confidence that he will not back down. As he was about to knock on the door, he noticed on each sides flower beds. Hmmm are those the flowers my dad grew? He thought. He smiled and knocked at the door. Unfortunately, like the first time, no one answered. He then knocked again, this time a little harder.

"Who is there?" A voice heard from inside.
"It is me Kristo, I came here last week."
"Haven't I told you not to come back?"
"Grand-father Kroople, please listen to me, I think I know something that might interest you."
"What is it that you know that I don't?"
"Give me five minutes and I will explain everything."

Silence stood.

About a minute later, he heard:
"You have five minutes."
Kristo took a deep breath and started reciting his observations which he had no too long ago to his father. Ending his story, and lifting some weight of his chest, he said:

"This is why I am here and I think that you have the answers to all this."

After some time, the door opened and he heard:
"Come in."

As he went in, Kristo saw a grand-father like he has never seen before. He had black fur only remaining on his back. The most part of his body was of a light-grey color. But what stood out the most was his long white beard that was almost touching the floor. With thick eyebrows of the same color. He was very skinny and hunched. You could not tell his age.

"You saw a fish," said the old one.

Kristo stood with a silly look on his face as if he had not heard what was said. Noticing it, the old one repeated himself.

"You saw a fish."

Only then, Kristo came to himself and unsurely asked:
"What is that?"
"I will tell you later," said the old Kroople. "But for now let's go step by step. And everything you see and hear will remain between us. For years I have been looking for someone to pass on my knowledge to and the values I protect which I inherited from my father which he did from his father and so on. But unfortunately I could not find anybody. Moreover, everybody I tried to share pieces of our history with did not believe me. I then decided that no one will ever hear a word from me."
"Do you promise?"
"I promise."
"According to your observations you feel that somewhere out there, there is another world."
"I think so, grand-father Kroople."
"You're right. It is unfortunate that during all this time we have lived here no one ever assumed that there was something beyond our world. Believe it or not, but this same place where you are currently sitting is just about a hundred of yards away from that other world."
"This cannot be!" exclaimed Kristo.
"When you were coming over here, did you notice that the street on which I live ends with a gigantic stone wall?"

"Yes I did."
"Behind that wall, you will find the other world."

Kristo was amazed. He thought he would run out of the old man's house towards the wall and break through. That is how much the words of the Old One excited him. Kroople noticed it and said:
"Calm down my son, it is still far from what you know and that is why you have to be ready to react normally."

After those words, Kristo regained his composure and with a confident tone asked:
"Yes but how do you know and what proof do you have?"

The old one looked at Kristo and after a short pause said:
"Do you see my bed?"
"Yes I see it."
"Go to it and move it away from the wall."

Kristo did so without much difficulty.

"Now, do you see the square rock in the corner?"
"I do."
-"Move it and bring me what is hidden behind it."

By moving the rock Kristo saw something he had never seen before. He simply took it and handed it to Kroople.
"What is it grand-father?" He asked.
"It is a book! It is the history of our people. It describes everything related to Kretonians throughout their long existence. But before opening it I need to ask you to blow the dust off of it."
"Of course."
By inhaling so deeply, Kristo blew so hard that a cloud of dust appeared around the old Kroople which tickled his nose and made him sneeze fivefold. It was funny and hard to watch.
"I am sorry," said Kristo. "I did not mean to make you sneeze."
"Don't worry, don't worry," said the old one.
But then, when the dust was gone, Kristo saw the image of a Kretonian and on the top he read "The history of Kretonia".
"Let's open it," said Kristo impatiently. "I want to read what's inside."

"No," said Kroople. "It is getting late and you have to leave. Come back another time or whenever you want but with one condition: you will read it by yourself.

This upset Kristo. The old one noticed and said:

"Understand me; I do not want your parents to suspect that you are coming home late." Asking you where you've been and what you have been doing.

You are right grand-father, said Kristo sighing.

But before you leave, push the bed back in place and put the book on the rock next to it.

Kristo did every thing he was asked, wished good night and went out.

Coming home he saw his father. Kristo knew that he was waiting for him to arrive.

Approaching him, Kristo could see the impatience in the look of his father. As if asking Kristo "What is today's result?". But Kristo, remembering the promise he has made, could only say hi. Wise enough at his age, Kerg easily noticed that Kristo came back that night completely different from last time. His eyes were sparkly and he was obviously concerned of something. His father decided not to question him about his visit but simply said:

"The supper is on the table and is still warm, go eat and get some rest.

" Thank you, but where is mother?

" She and Kerta went to visit grand-mother Klida. She got suddenly sick so mother decided to bring her a herbal beverage. But they will come back soon.

Having finished his supper, Kristo went to bed right away. Hoping to have a chance to hear something else from, father sat not far away from him. They remained this way for some time without saying a word. Kristo's situation was a bit complicated because he already saw and knew something. He saw the impatience in his father and it bothered him. Struggling by the fact, Kristo finally said:

" I am sorry father, but I made the promise I would not tell anyone and please understand me.

"I understand son, but if ever you need help I will be glad to help you.

" Thank you very much. And if you don't mind I would like to use it right now.

" I am listening , said the father with a smile.

The situation is that I will have to go to the old Kroople every day. But there is a little problem.
" Name it.
" You know that I work almost every day all day.
" Of course.
" This is why I would like to change my schedule and only work half of a day so I can meet with Kroople and come back home for supper so that mother would not suspect anything. I would not like her to know anything. You know how sensitive she is.
" Yes, yes of course. For that you can count on me. Regarding your work, you should speak with the head of the mill.
"I have already thought about it. I don't think I will have any problems.
" Every thing is alright then, sleep tight.
Before wishing his father good night, Kristo said one more thing:
" Nothing is as simple as it seemed dad.
" That is what I am starting to think, replied Kerg; good night son.
" Good night dad.

Walking away, Kerg felt that the worries in his heart have increased. When Mother and Kerta finally came back, Kristo was deeply asleep.
In the morning, Kristo arrived to work earlier than usually and immediately looked for the head of the mill.
" Mr. Klinsson (that is how every body would call him), do you have a minute to talk to me?
" Yes, yes of coarse Kristo. Did anything happened?
" No, nothing happened. I simply wanted to ask your permission to change my schedule only for a couple of days.
" What can I do for you Kristo?
" I need to free the second half of my day.
Every body knew Mr. Klinsson was a Kretonian of few words who did not ask many questions and was very benevolent.
And he answered: - No problem.
" But if you want I can ask my friend Korry to replace me, he has worked here before.
" No, no, and no, protested Mr. Klinsson. I remember him very well. He has worked here for only a day and held my guys from working because of his humour. Thank you, maybe some other time.
" May I begin starting tomorrow?
" It's a deal.

On the next day, first thing finishing work, he ran to the river to wash the dust off himself left by the bags of flour and at the same time refresh himself. After a quick dry on the shore, he proceeded to meet with Kroople. The old one had a feeling Kristo would come as he was waiting for him at the door.

" Here you are. I knew you would come. Come in, but first grab something to eat. I am sure you haven't had lunch.

" Thank you grand-father Kroople, but I am not hungry. Instead let's hurry and open the book.

" How impatient you are, but I will not insist. Bring it here.

And together they sat at the table.

" If you have any question, I will gladly answer, said the old one.

Kristo anxiously and slowly opened the book. He shortly paused and read out loud afraid to skip a word.

The first chapter described their origins, that hundreds and hundreds years ago they derived from the wolf. It was accompanied by illustrations on which depicted a quite big beast. For comparison, in the corner of the page was a page of a three-hundred year old Kretonian. The ancestor seemed three times bigger. The fur was as black but much thicker. He looked like a fearless warrior with a proud bearing. Kristo then noticed the ears and the fact that they were both identical.

" Grand-father Kroople, what happened to our ears since the ancestors' are completely triangle?

" There is only one suggestion my dear. Many thought that through hundreds of years of development of Kretonians, their bodies transformed and therefore something affected our ears. But it is something none could explain. I will jump ahead and say that no one figured out the mystery of our tails. We are the only ones with fiery tails. But read on said the old Kroople.

Kristo got to the evolution chapter. It did not contain much material but on one of the pages was another illustration on which three Kretonians were drawn. The first was exactly like we saw on the first page. Under him was written "2000 years ago". The other one was half as big and had less fur. Under him was written "1000 years ago". And the last one was a Kretonian not different from the present. "300 years ago" was written.

" This is so interesting, said Kristo.

When he turned the page, a beautiful view opened to his eyes. But unfortunately he did not know what it was.

" What is this? asked Kristo.
" This is the other world. Do you see the blue streak on the top? It's the sky. It is endless. In this corner something yellow spreads - it is the sun. It keeps that world warm. Everything you see on the bottom is called earth. Do you see how many different things grow on it, trees, flowers, bushes. Kristo was listening with his mouth wide open.
" But now get ready, said the old one.
" Do you see the mountain afar and the river not far from it?
" Yes, I do see it, answered Kristo.
" It is that same mountain under which you are living and that same river in which you swim.

Kristo was staring at the illustration speechless and for a few minutes he sat motionless.

"Are you alright Kristo?" Asked the old Kroople; slightly pushing him.

Only then he came back to his senses and asked in a dry voice:
"Can I have some water please?"

The old one laughed and pointed to the pitcher of water sitting on the table. Kristo had probably never drunk so much water in his life. As he finished drinking, he splashed a bit on his face, snorted, and turned around to Kroople who was sitting happily and smiling. He knew he found the one he had been looking for, for so long.

"Are you ready to go even further?" asked the old one.
"I think it is enough for today," answered Kristo. I would rather go home, I need some time to think about everything I saw and read today.
"I agree with you, but when will you come back?"
"Same time tomorrow."
"I'll be waiting."

After Kristo had left the house, Kroople decided to leave everything untouched. He warmed up his herbal beverage, drank it with pleasure, and decided to go to bed.

"The sooner I go to bed, the sooner I will wake up and the sooner Kristo will come back," thought the old one.

For Kristo, it was the first sleepless night in his life. He could see the book in his eyes, especially the page where he saw the mountain.

The next morning, Kristo got out of bed but made sure not to show his fatigue so that his mother would not suspect anything.
As if nothing had happened, he had breakfast and headed to work. Passing by the river, he thought: - If I dive in it, then nothing should happen. He slowly walked into the water. Spending a few minutes inside, Kristo felt his good mood and cheerfulness come back. Coming out of the water, he started singing one of the many Kretonian songs and headed to the mill. This day was not different from any other, other than the fact that Kristo put more effort into his work than he usually did. Noticing this, Mr. Klinsson approached him and thanked him.
"Thank you very much," said Kristo as he ran to the river to refresh himself.

Exactly at the arranged meeting time, they were both sitting at the table and Kristo turned the next page. On the next page, he saw many different kinds of animals and some who even like him.
"Grand-father Kroople, I need your help again. Who are they? And where do they live?"
"They are those who inhabit the country of Veldronia. They are also illustrated on three other pages. There are many of them but they all live peacefully. This, for example, is a wolf. Does he remind you of anyone?"
"Yes of course, he looks a lot like us!"
"Well there he is, your ancient ancestor."
"This is a squirrel which lives on trees and runs on branches so fast that it is very hard to catch. This is a mole; he lives underground but not as deep as us. This is an eagle; it's a bird and it flies very high in that same sky which you saw on the previous page.
"What does flying mean?

The old Kroople reflected for a bit and then said:
"I will try to recreate what they do, but I am unsure since I, myself have never seen it. My father once showed it to me, but it was a long time ago."

With a lot of difficulty, he stood up on his back paws and flapped with his frontal ones up and down.

Kristo could hardly resist bursting into laughter. But the old one noticed it.

"I know I look ridiculous but that is the only way I know how to show you," he said.

"No, no, of course not!" said Kristo avoiding eye contact.

"Alright, alright, I might be old but I am not blind," said Kroople. "But let's continue. Do you recognize who that is?"

"Isn't this what I saw in the river" asked Kristo.

"Yes, I already told you, you saw a fish, remember?"

"Of course I remember".

"Some jump, some run, some fly, but she swims."

"What does swimming mean?"

But the old one did not answer and looked at him suspiciously. At that moment, Kristo stared at the ceiling with his head turned, smiling.

"If you think I will imitate a fish, then don't count on it," said the old one.

"Of course not, I can imagine how they do it. Let's keep looking."

And Kristo saw many different kinds of animals which the old Kroople explained to him in detail.

The last illustration on the third page was a weird looking and a very horrendous creature.

"Who is this?" asked Kristo. "This creature does not look like anyone."

"They are our neighbours that live on the other side of the entrance. You've probably heard of them."

"Yes of course, from the conversations I've had with my dad. He told me there is a tunnel in one of the walls and if you go through you will find yourself on a stone plain where those creatures live. He strongly ordered me to never go there."

"Your father is right, since he has to take care of you. But here is what I would like to tell you son; their looks are very frightful and anyone who would see them up close would begin to tremble. But that is not all true. They are actually harmless. They just live their lives. They don't eat anything and only drink water from the same river we do."

"How do you know they are harmless?"

"You see, I am very old now and cannot trek for long distances, but I used to go there quite often and have never seen them behave aggressively. I used to go there simply by curiosity. I would sit on the shore and observe them and I would sometimes think; it's good that at least someone lives close. They never paid attention to my presence. After drinking water, they would raise their noses out of the water and make what seemed to me terrifying sounds at that time. But then I got used to them and came to realize that it was how they expressed their emotions. I will now reveal to you a secret. It happened that they were the ones who showed us they way to the same place where we currently live.

"Wait grand-father, wait," interrupted Kristo. "My head is spinning. What does it mean, they showed us the way? What does that wolf mean - ancestor? From what I understand, he lived in that other world with everybody else; which means we also came from there."

Kroople looked at him affectionately and simply said:

"Just a little bit more and you will find out about everything, be patient."

"Alright, but just tell me, what are those creatures called, the ones that live on the plains, and where do they come from."

"We used to call them Montronoses but as the years passed, Kretonians began to forget about their existence and the only thing that was left was their name; monster. How they got here, no one knows."

"That is unfortunate," whispered Kristo.

"Now we have approached to the answer to your question," said the old one turning the page.

Turning the page, Kristo read at the top "Life of a Kretonian". This part consisted of twenty full pages. The description of their lives was accompanied with pictures. At the very beginning was described how a long time ago, in cold lands, a group of animals was formed. They lived in very small dwellings in the shape of pyramids made out of thick layers of branches. At the center of each dwelling was a place for a fire which they had to sustain almost all year long. It was not hard for them since a simple touch of their tails would light up the dry leaves and branches. In one of the dwellings that was illustrated on the picture you could see two of them cuddling together and two others playing something. They nourished themselves with nuts, wild berries and small roots. The following description showed how fast their community grew. On another image, you could see how a new group of those creatures arrived and was warmly welcomed.

Furthermore, as you got to know Kretonians a little better, you could see how their level of life elevated. The houses got larger and more comfortable and next to every house you could see a garden. An illustration showing two Kretonians telling each other something amusing, showed their much augmented level of intellectuality.

More was ahead.

Kristo read continuously and Kroople had to even remind him to breath. On one of the pages was a big portrait on which a mature Kretonian was illustrated with a wise look on his face. He had a thick and long moustache which differentiated him from the rest. On the bottom you could read "Kitton".

"Who is this?" asked Kristo.

"It is our first leader. He is the one who gathered and united us together. Thanks to him, Kretonians moved from cold to warm lands where they lived for a long time."

"What happened next?" wondered Kristo.

"Keep reading and you will find out," answered Kroople.

On the next page, Kristo found out that Kitton brought them together where other animals inhabited which was yet to see in this book. On this page he saw, a cat, a dog, a hamster, a donkey, a rabbit and many other animals.

The old one then interrupted him.

"Do you see the big gathering of animals on the next page?"

"Yes, I see," replied Kristo.

"It is on this gathering that the name of our country and population was created.

To the question of one of the leaders of what would be the name of our country would be, someone replied: "Kretonia!". After a short silence, the crowed began to shout: KRETONIA, KRETONIA, KRETONIA!"

-"Since then we have been called Kretonians," said the old one. "Everybody else around us are also called Kretonians. The history says that it was the best time in which we all lived together, built, cultivated crops, learned, helped each other, visited each other and celebrated."

And all of a sudden, the old one ceased speaking as if something scared him."

"What happened, grand-father?"

"Nothing, everything is alright, keep reading," said the old one in a weeping voice.

The next two pages described exactly what Kristo had just heard. He then turned to Kroople and asked him:

"Whose example should I follow?"

"Forgive me, the elderly too can sometimes be impatient," he answered looking away.

Kristo looked at him with love and thought of how grateful he was to his father for sending him here. Kristo learnt more and more from what he was reading but came the time to turn the next page. As soon as he was about to do this, he heard a heavy sigh from the old one. Kristo turned to him and noticed how Kroople had instantly changed. His snow-white eyebrows and moustache lowered and tears appeared in his gloomy eyes.

"Grand-father, what happened?" asked Kristo frightfully.

"Nothing, nothing," he said. "We just got to the part of the book where they talk about the sorrow that has come upon us and it is always hard for me as my heart bleeds when I get to this part, but you keep reading."

And Kristo turned another page.

On it, he saw a humongous black cat with narrow eyes of a bright-red color. You would think that fire burned inside them. He was sitting in a big chair with the look of the cruellest creature. On each side, loathsome creatures were standing with long noses under which two yellow fangs stuck out. Their claws weren't any shorter and they had long whiskers and long bald tails. Their iron helmets would differentiate them from those who were standing behind them.

Kristo was ready to turn the page but in that moment Kroople grabbed him by the shoulder.

"Listen," he said. "I certainly know that it is interesting for you to know who these awful creatures are and what happened next, but let's put the book aside for now. I would like to go on further myself. I think I would feel better if I recited the following events myself."

Kristo did not argue and slowly closed the book and pushed it aside.

"The one you see in the chair is called Dezmort, he is the one who brought all the misfortunes to Kretonians. He possesses magical powers. Slightly opening his eyes and looking at someone is enough to kill someone. Those two you saw on his sides were at the time his chief commanders. They are rats. They are the most merciless creatures. Especially Dezmort, with the help of these two and a whole army, conquered our country."

"But where did they come from?" asked Kristo.

"The book says they came from the other side of the ocean but no one knows for sure from which country and everywhere they went, they left misfortunes behind them. When they reached the walls of our city, we were not prepared to fight back and they easily defeated us. Though that does not mean we did not fight back. We fought against them in every wall of the city, on every street, in any place. But the strengths were unfair. Many courageous Kretonians have fallen since no one ever taught them how to fight. We lived with everybody in peace but that day ended everything for us. Dezmort declared himself as Lord of Kretonia and demanded full dependence to him. As a result of disobedience, death was awaiting. We could only give in. On the second day, he ordered to assemble the whole community and declared that as of the day after, every native will begin the construction of a colossal castle in which he decided to live eternally. The next morning at sun rise, the whole population of Kretonia began building the castle. Some worked at the quarry, some hauled the stones and others erected the walls. The work was very hard having only a short moment to rest during the day. Dezmort's soldiers were all over the place. If someone fell or slowed down of fatigue, rat would run up to him and start beating him."

"But grand-father Kroople, no one lives forever."

"Absolutely," answered the old one and sighed again. You see Kristo, in this Despot, hearts are absent and that magic power makes him think that he is immortal indeed."

"There must be something that can destroy him."

"Yes of course."

"Then name it."

"It is not something, it is someone. I do not know who it is but he must be very wise, strong and a very courageous warrior," said Kroople.

"And what does he have to do in order to defeat him?"

"Be patient, and listen to me until the end," said the old one.

The thing is, even though he does not seem to have a heart it does not necessarily mean that he doesn't have one. He does have one but he hid it very far from here. It is preserved in a crystal chest which lies on a high marble table. Under the table hangs a sword on two golden chains. Only who masters this sword will be able to crush Dezmort's heart. However it is guarded in one of the caves by three huge rattle snakes."

"Where is that?" asked Kristo.

"It is in a hot country very far away, where strange spiky trees grow."

"Tell me grand-father, what does one have to do in order to destroy the heart?"

"First you need to kill the snakes, then bring it to the city and split his heart in two before his eyes. Only then will his existence come to an end."

After these words, Kristo lowered his head and Kroople noticed how wide he had spread his paws. As sharp his claws appeared, Kristo was breathing heavily. You could hear him gritting his teeth."

After some time, Kristo stared at the old one and said:

"How come in so long no one has been able to reach to the heart and destroy it?"

"There were four of them son," replied Kroople. "But Dezmort's spies had revealed the plot. Three of them were captured and executed in front of everybody. The fourth one escaped and managed to get to the cave. But the snakes were waiting for him and so they ended his life."

Kristo became silent again. Only after a few moments he was able to say: "How cruel…"

"Grand-father Kroople, before I leave, I would like to ask you one more question."

"I'm listening."

"How did we end up living so deep underground and not stay there with everybody else?"

"On the third day of his ruling, Dezmort ordered to exile us from the country. He gave us two days to get our things and leave. During this time he ordered his soldiers to find a "suitable" place for us. Two days later, we were gathered together and escorted by the rats out of the city. At night, we were brought to the mountain where we were pointed to the narrow entrance. One of the commanders ordered us to get in one by one and go to the very bottom. It is one by one that we vanished and never came out of there."

"What about the rats, didn't they follow you down there?"

"No they were scared of the sounds that were coming from the depths of the mountain." As for parting words, the commander said: "If you try to escape from this cave, you will suffer a brutal death".

At the head walked our leader, he was the first to walk down and was the first who saw a Montronose. Both froze and stared at each other but our leader was very brave and was able to withstand the Montronose's stare. At that moment, more Kretonians joined the leader's side and circled him to show that they were ready to defend their leader and would not back down. The Montronose seemed to understand, so after a short reflection, he pointed to us the path we had to follow. He then raised his nose and uttered a horrible sound. Only then we understood what it meant. That was the way he expressed his welcoming to us. As Kretonians followed their path, the book describes their silent movement trying to get through the narrow passage without making too much noise as the Montronoses stopped and stared at them. Quite often, they would utter their noises which gave Kretonians cold chills. After crossing the river, we found ourselves in front of those same corridors which lead us here where we have been living ever since."

"But why, why did we get exiled?" asked Kristo in a trembling voice.

"There are only assumptions to your questions my dear. Many came to the conclusion that it is because of our tails which spread some fear on the rats. They always looked at them with mistrust and revealed their teeth whenever one of us would get near accidentally. We think it is the chief commanders of Dezmort who succeeded in obtaining what they wanted, our exile."

Kristo shook his head and then sat and stared for quite some time. Standing up with a dispirited look, he said:

"It's time for me to go."

"When will you come back?" asked Kroople.

"I don't know. Soon I think."

And he left leaving the old one alone.

When he was walking back home, different feelings were fighting in his thoughts and he thought his head would burst. The degradation and the exile of Kretonians caused him a lot of grief. His emotions then turned into hate towards Dezmort and his servants. You could see how his tears became a merciless snarl. It is in this condition that he slowly reached his house and it is only in front of the front door that came to his senses."

"I need to take control of myself," said Kristo to himself. "No one must suspect my condition."

Opening the door, he went in.

This time father was not home.

"Where's dad?" asked Kristo.

"He went to see his friends," answered mother while setting the table.

"How is work?" she asked. "You don't look too good, have you gotten sick by any chance?"

"No, I'm just really tired today. Do you mind if I go for a short walk after supper?"

"Sure, go ahead, a walk always helps relieve fatigue.

At this moment Kerta ran up.

I thought you would play with me today," she said. "We haven't played together in such a long time and it is unfair," said his little sister .

"I am sorry my dear, but I promise I'll play with you all night long tomorrow, deal?"

"Alright," said Kerta.

At that moment the door opened and father came in.

He looked at his son with a fixed gaze. Making eye contact with his father, Kristo quickly looked away.

And this time, father knew it was unnecessary to ask questions.

"Hi," said Kerg.

"Hi dad."

Right after supper, Kristo headed to see Kliko. He thought he needed to be in good company to relax. After meeting with him they headed to see Korry but he was not home. His mother said that he went to the abandoned quarry with two other friends.

"Awesome!" said Kliko. "We haven't been there in a while."

Wishing Korry's mother a good-night, they headed to the quarry.

Getting there, not only did they see their three friends but five other young Kretonians. A competition was under way and and there was nothing left for Kristo and Kliko but to join them. The competition consisted of three events. As usual Kroopo won the first one, in which the competitor had to run and jump as far as possible. Korry tried to disturb him but nothing would work and Kroopo became champion. The second event consisted of a jumping competition. Surprisingly, Kayoor was the one who jumped the highest.

"What happened to you?" said Korry. "You probably haven't had supper today and happened to be the lightest of us all." Everybody laughed. As everybody expected, Kristo won the third event. A heavy stone weighing around twenty pounds had to be lifted and brought across a designated line. The only one that was the closest to Kristo's record was Kliko but even he did not make it through the last quarter of the distance. Two others were only able to lift the stone dropping it back down.

"How does he do it? It is so heavy!" they asked each other.

After the competition and after a short rest, they all headed to the river.

On his way, Kristo thought that it was a good idea that he join his friends to spend some time with them. A minute later, he felt very tired. At least he will have a good sleep, he thought.

After the swim, lying on the shore, everybody thought it was time to head home.

As he got home, Kristo went right to his room, let himself fall on the bed and closed his eyes right away. He heard his father walk up to him and cover him with a blanket after which he fell asleep. He dreamt of Kretonians gathered together, crying and hugging their kids as the rats were walking around a chattering their teeth. Dezmort was sitting on top of his castle and laughing maliciously. He saw them being chased away out of their town with smashing clubs. He saw how the last Kretonian disappeared in the cave. He also saw Kitton who approached him, put his paw on his shoulder and pronounced: "Only you".

Kristo felt like someone was shaking him by the very same shoulder. He hardly opened his eyes and saw his father.

"Good morning son, it's time to wake up breakfast is on the table. Eat and go to work because you are running late and I have to bring Kerta to daycare."

"See you," answered Kristo.

After a quick breakfast, he ran out of the house in the direction of the mill. He got there when the first carrier had already put a bag on his shoulder. All day long, Kristo thought of the dream he had that night. Especially the part where Kitton approached him. All day long, he could hear the two words that were said to him: "Only you". Later, he did not even notice how he kept answering to those words out loud: "Only me". Dropping his last bag, forgetting all the other carriers around him, he pronounced out loud with a lot of determination: "Only me!" The ones around him looked at each other surprised. Someone then jokingly shouted:

"Of course you! Who else?"
As it made everybody laugh.

Confused, Kristo hurried to leave.
As he had promised, he devoted that night to Kerta. She was reciting him the new poems she had learned at the daycare. She sang him a new song. Then started playing Tic Tac Toe and Kristo, as a good and kind older brother, was giving in. Every win would bring the little sister a lot of joy.
"I won again! I won again!" Kerta shouted mockingly while sticking her tongue out.
But Kristo was just laughing.
"Good, good! You are the smart one, but that's enough for today it is time for you to go to bed.".

Happy with her victories, Kerta headed to her bed hopping and singing something to herself. A few minutes later, Kristo could hear her smooth breathing.

That night, Kerg and Kvila were invited for supper and so were a little bit late. Kristo was once again left alone with his thoughts.
After a short reflection, he came to the conclusion that he needed to see the old Kroople once again. He needed to share his decision about him leaving the town and engaging in a battle with Dezmort. Kristo was hoping to get good advice from him. Without him thinking he could dissuade Kristo. Everything was settled.
He then remembered his parents and his heart started to hurt. I cannot just tell them: "I am leaving you and don't know when I'll be back" he thought. I have to disappear without saying a word." How to solve this problem?
After a long reflection without answers, Kristo thought of asking Kroople for advice about this as well, after which he went to sleep.

The next day, after work and a quick bite, Kristo left his house and rapidly rushed to see the old one.
Kvila did not even have time to ask him anything.
"Listen dear," she turned to her husband. "Don't you get the feeling that our son has changed? That he has shrunk into himself and has become a man of few words?"
Kerg was ready for this question as he knew one day it would come up and had prepared what seemed to him a logic answer.

"You know dear, I think our son is simply in love," he said cunningly trying to keep eye-contact.

As he suspected, he was believed.

"No way! How did you know?"

"Think for yourself Kvila. In the last few days he became reticent as you have noticed, to me he seems a little bit excited, and he is always rushing somewhere. It reminds me of myself when I met you."

After which Kerg approached Kvila with a smile and gave her a kiss on the nose.

"Do you know her?" excitingly asked Kvila.

"Unfortunately not."

"This is good news!" exclaimed Kvila. "I am now reassured."

As she went on to clean around the house, Kerg looked at her with a lot of sympathy.

It is good that she does not know anything but even I don't know anything yet, he thought. Only mixed and unpromising thoughts were circulating in his head.

This time, Kristo had probably beat the record in the longest distance ran. All wet and out of breath, he did not slow down but just stopped right at Kroople's door.

After taking a few deep breaths and barely regaining his proper breathing, he knocked at the door.

As the old Kroople saw him, he became confused.

"Have you run Kretonia three times?" asked the old one.

Kristo did not answer. He went right to the pitcher of water. After drinking probably half of it, he deeply sighed. He stood there for another minute and when he completely regained his breathing he answered:

"Not less than five times probably."

"Alright, so tell me what's going on?"

"I came here to tell you that I have decided to go back up and help the ones that are still there. Please do not try to dissuade me."

Kroople stared at Kristo as if paralyzed. After a short pause, Kristo noticed it and whispered:

"Are you alright grand-father?"

The question helped the grand-father come back to reality.

"Kristo, you have lost your mind! You know what will happen to you if you get caught by those rats. And what can you do alone, not having any friends, and not knowing what is going on up there at the moment? How are you planning on fighting?"

"I will find some friends! I am not afraid to go there because I know what awaits me!" And how I am planning on fighting? I think everything will happen on the spot and I asked you not to try to change my mind."

"I am not trying to dissuade you. I see it is hard to change your mind. I am simply worrying about you."

After these words, Kroople got up with difficutly and started walking back and forth with a frown.

Kristo was just looking at the old one's movements.

After some time, the old one stopped next to Kristo and looking him in the eyes seriously asked:

"When are you planning to?"

"I am thinking in a few days. I want to spend more time with my parents and sister."

The old one nodded his head in agreement.

"But I need your advice," said Kristo.

-"I don't know what to do with my parents. I can't just tell them that I am leaving them, maybe even forever."

The old one stopped to think. After a few minutes, he said:

"Leave it up to me. Since I am the one who started this and I will be the one to blame."

"How will you do that?"

"I don't know yet, but I'm hoping for the best. You have to trust me in everything."

"I completely trust you grand-father."

After that, Kristo felt a weight lift off his shoulders.

They then sat together silently without saying a word.

"Alright," finally said Kristo after some time. "It is time for me to go."

"Wait," said the old one. "Promise me that right before your departure you will come see me."

-"I promise," said Kristo as he left.

While he was walking back home, he decided to leave on his long journey in three days.

Closing the door behind Kristo, old Kroople went to bed. It was not easy for him. He then thought of what he would tell Kristo's parents and how they would react to what he would say. I don't have a choice, he thought. I will tell them the whole truth and hope they will understand us both.

After which he got on his bed and took out a small chest off the shelf. After blowing the dust off, he carefully opened it and observed its contents for a while.

Kristo spent all his remaining days with his parents and sister. He was trying to look happy and calm. He did not refuse even once to play with Kerta. After supper, at the table, Kristo would tell funny stories about what happened that day at the mill. The parents had noticed the change.
"Dear, don't you find Kristo has changed in the past two days?" asked Kvila.
"I also see it but I don't know what to think."

Kerg was really confused but at the same time he thought a weight came off his shoulders.
"Maybe Kristo got his first kiss," playfully proposed Kvila with a smile.
"You might be right," replied Kerg also with a smile and gave her a kiss.

Everything continued this way for another day.

The next morning after breakfast, Kristo behaved the same way he had in the past three days. He only had a minute left before going to "work". He approached Kerta and gave her a few big kisses on the nose only telling her, "goodbye sister". He then approached his mother and gave her a very big kiss.
"I love you very much mommy," he said as he looked in her eyes for an instant and quickly looked away.
Kvila was left motionless. As he approached his father and looked at him with love, he firmly said: - I'll see you soon dad.
As he got out of the house, he closed the door and stood for a while. His heart was bleeding thinking he might never see them again.
He walked and cried thinking of them as he suddenly bumped into Kliko and Korry turning the corner.
"Hi Kristo!" they both shouted.
"Hi guys."
"Are you going to the mill?" asked Kliko.
"Yes."
"Will you join us at the river after work?"
"Of course, as always."
"See you tonight then!"

"See you tonight," answered Kristo as they parted ways.

"Did you notice anything?" Kliko suspiciously asked Korry.
"Yes, I think something has happened.
"I've never seen Kristo with such teary eyes. The mill isn't that way either."
"Let's follow him," suggested Kliko. "Maybe he needs help?"
"Let's," answered Korry as they follow their friend from a distance without losing sight of him.

Kristo brought them to the old Kroople's house.
"Do you know who lives here?" asked Korry.
"I have no clue, let's go hide behind that rock and see what happens," suggested Kliko.
"Good idea," agreed Korry.

When Kristo entered the house, he did not recognise the old one. He had changed a lot in those past few days. It looked as if he aged another fifty years. He was even more bent over and was moving at an even slower pace than before.
"Come in," barely pronounced Kroople. "So, you haven't changed your mind yet?"
"No."
The old one raised his head high and said:
"I am proud of you! And we will all be proud of you! But before you leave I have to give you something that now only belongs to you."
He brought Kristo to the table on which rested the chest.
"Open it and take out what lays inside."
Kristo carefully lifted the lid, and at the bottom saw a big silver medallion on a thick chain. After taking it out, he started examining it. At the center he saw the image of someone he had already seen in the book. It was Kitton. What he saw made his mouth drop open. He had never held anything like it in his life.
"This medallion always belonged to our leader and it is now yours. Put it on! It will guard you!"
Anxiously shaking, Kristo put his head through and froze.
Only then, looking at this young and strong Kretonian, Kroople did not regret anything. He saw standing in front of him a courageous and proud warrior.

"Your time has come," said the old one.

Kristo nodded his head, stood next to Kroople and said:

"We will definitely see each other again."

As he almost got to the mysterious corridor, he heard behind him: - Kristo!

When he turned around he froze because in front of him stood Kliko and Korry.

Even before he had time to come back to himself, Kliko firmly asked him:

"Where are you going and what is that on your chest?"

Kristo did not find an answer right away. His thoughts were mixed. The only thing that came to his mind was:

"Nowhere, just taking a walk here."

"Don't lie," said Korry.

"We know you are heading to this corridor."

Kristo understood that lying was useless.

"Yes, you guessed it. I just want to see the Montronoses that live on the other side."

"Then we'll come with you," said Kliko.

They proceeded with determination towards the corridor and seeing that, Kristo quickly cut them off.

"You won't go there," said Kristo strictly.

"You cannot tell us where we cannot go. We can go anywhere we want."

Kristo understood that arguing is also useless. After a short pause he said:

"My friends, you know how much I love you, but I really need you to believe with me. I cannot tell you anything at the moment, I promised and I have to go there alone. The time will come when you'll find out about everything. But now please leave."

They looked at each other for a long time. Kliko then said:

"Alright but promise that if ever you need help you will call us to help you."

The friends waited until their friend vanished in the corridor then turned around and walked in the opposite way.

Having walked a bit, Kliko was the first to break the silence:

"I want to know more about all of this!"

"Me too," confirmed Korry.

Exchanging glances, they understood each other

Kristo was not walking but sneaking through the corridor. Coming out of it, he tucked in his tail not to give himself away. Peering ahead, he saw the river which Kroople had told him about. All of a sudden, fifty yards away from him, he saw those monsters.

Seven or eight of them were gathered together and were drinking water on slow intervals. Carefully looking, Kristo saw another Montronose. He was standing apart from the group. Kristo then decided to get near the river, close to the place where the lonely monster was sitting. He noticed that not far from him, rested a big enough stone behind which he could hide. Without making any noise, Kristo ran up and hid behind it. He suddenly realized he did not feel any fear but instead some sort of interest and a sense of adventure that was taking over. He then peaked from behind the rock and he noticed that Montronose was half as big as the others. "He is probably a young one," thought Kristo to himself. "But he is the one I need." Finding a little stone, Kristo threw it in the direction where sat the Montronose. The rock fell right in front of his nose. He was not expecting it and he quickly looked up. Flashing his fiery eyes, he emitted a displeased but quiet roar. After looking around and not seeing anything, he plunged his nose back in the water.

Kristo then waited a bit before throwing a second stone which landed at the same place as the first one.

The Montronose lifted his head once again but did not emit any sound and just looked around.

Kristo came out from behind the rock and quietly called him:

"Hey, hey, I'm here."

Noticing him, the Montronose got up on his rear legs and was ready to emit an awful roar until he saw Kristo's desperate paws waving and covering his own mouth. He seemed to understand that Kristo did not want to make any noise as he sat waiting to see what would happen next.

Kristo rejoiced at the fact that everything happened quietly and headed forward. Jumping from rock to rock and sometimes getting in the water, he reached the other shore. Coming out of the water, the Kretonian approached the Montronose from the side where he could not be seen by others and quietly said:

"I am Kristo, what is your name?"

There was no answer.

"They probably can't speak," thought Kristo scratching behind his ear. All of a sudden he heard:

"I am Juba."

His voice seemed to come from the inside.

"You are probably one of those who live on the other side of the wall?" asked the monster.

"Yes. My people and I do live there."

"What are you looking for?" with the same guttural voice he asked.

Kristo sat across and after a short pause replied:

"Listen, my friend, it happened that from the tales of an old Kretonian, I found out that here, where you live, is an exit which leads to another world."

"I don't know what you mean by another world but there is definitely a big hole which goes high above. We are forbidden to enter it."

"That is exactly what I am looking for!" said Kristo with excitement. "Could you bring me there?"

-After a short reflection, Juba got up on his legs and with a nod of his head invited him to follow.

"Just follow the right side as I do not want us to be seen together."

During the whole walk, they did not utter a word. Juba did not pay any attention to him. After a certain time he suddenly stopped.

"What happened?" asked Kristo.

"I am sorry I cannot go any further. You will have to continue on your own."

"But where?"

"Walk along this wall and it will lead you to that place you are looking for. It's not far from here."

For a moment, Kristo remembered what the old one told him; that the monsters living on this side aren't angry at all and that have even helped the Kretonians. He then turned to Juba and gratefully said:

"Thank you my friend. I will never forget that."

"You are welcome and if ever you need help, you know where to look for me. Good luck."

After making a few steps forward, Kristo looked back. Juba was still standing at the same place.

"We'll meet again!" shouted the Kretonian
.

The Montronose just raised his nose and emitted the scary sound.

The hole was not too far indeed and standing in front of it, Kristo noticed that it was not that small. "An adult size Montronose could get through," he thought. Kristo did not reflect for too long.

"Ahead!" he said to himself as he went in.

Using his tail as a torch, Kristo moved through with determination taking only one short break. He did not feel any fear and as he then thought, he did not feel any hunger.

Right at that moment, Kvila was finishing preparing supper.

"Where is Kristo?" he seems to be running late today, she noticed.

"I think he will arrive soon," answered Kerg.

But Kristo did not show up.

Having finished their supper, mother and father sat down together to discuss how the day went by and the latest news. Suddenly, a few knocks were heard at the door.

"I will get that," said Kerg with a frown.

The old Kroople was standing on the porch. A thought hit hit father but he did not show it.

"Hello, my name is Kroople and I would like to have a talk with you."

"Hello, come in. My wife and I would be happy to talk with you."

"No, no, thank you but I cannot come in right now. I came here to talk to only you and if it's possible. Let's find a quiet place near the river where I will explain everything." At that moment, Kerg new that something serious had happened and his heart began to beat even faster.

"Yes, yes of course. I know the perfect place," he said in a worried voice.

Arriving there, they sat next to one another. Kerg noticed how the old one lowered his head. He was waiting.

Kroople took time to begin and after gathering his strengths, he pronounced;
"I came to see you to ask for your forgiveness."
Kerg was silent.
"I know that Kristo did not come home today and it is my fault. I know that he will not be back tomorrow either but if you let me, I will explain what has happened."
After these words, Kerg lowered his head. A strong feeling of anxiety remained in his heart. In such a condition, he finally pronounced:
"Tell me everything please."
The old man nodded his head and began explaining to Kerg how he met Kristo and how he introduced him to his book. About the legends described inside; about the silver medallion which he had handed to Kristo; everything from the beginning to the end.
Kerg did not move and never interrupted him.
When Kroople finished, he simply said:
"Forgive me please."

After a few minutes, Kristo's father raised his head and looking at old Kroople said:
"Do not blame yourself. I am responsible for all this. It was me who told him about you and told him that you knew stories and legends. I just thought that Kristo wanted to learn something and had no idea he would react this way. I now realize I was wrong. But what is going to happen now? What am I supposed to do?"
"Wait and have faith," answered Kroople.
Kerg lowered his head again and stared in into thin air. He was confused.
It was a pity for Kroople to see Kerg in this condition. The facial expression of Kristo's father suddenly changed.
"Mr. Kerg, I understand your feelings, but believe me when I tell you that my heart hurts just as much. After all the time I spent with your son, I realized that he became to me the most precious person in my life and now I want you to look at me please."
Kerg heavily raised his head and looked at the old Kroople.
"Believe me Mr. Kerg, Kristo will be back. I know it."
Tears appeared on Kerg's face but the words of the old Kroople had a significant influence on him and he calmed down a bit. After a short pause, he said:

"This is probably destiny and there is nothing we can do about it. As you said, we just have to wait and have faith."

"Dear Kerg, I am quite old already and I have seen enough throughout my entire life, but I want you to know that a person like your son Kristo and I who have only a couple of times once. I can confidently tell you are proud of him. The time will come indeed, when the entire Kretonia will be proud of him."

Once again, tears appeared on Kerg's face. He did not know what to say. He was overwhelmed. He sat a bit, until his eyes dried, and with a low tone said:

"I have to go and thank you for not hiding anything from us."

Kroople did not answer. He just watched Kerg as he was leaving. He then stiffly got up and went in the opposite way."

"He is the happiest father," said Kroople to himself.

On his way home, Kerg kept thinking about what he would tell Kvila.
- "I have no choice but to tell her the truth, there is nothing else I can do. Let it be."

Getting through the tunnel without too much trouble, Kristo arrived in a large room that we have visited before. In the very poor lighting he came to realize that it was quite an ordinary place; just damp and gloomy. Suddenly, he noticed a specific place in the room where something bright was penetrating through. By intuition he head in that direction. The closer he was getting, the brighter it became around him. He felt that he was on the right path.

"Another world, another very exciting world," he whispered several times to himself.

And in an instance, he literally stood before this "other world".

Out of such an unexpected bright light, Kristo automatically shut his eyes. He was not ready for it. Eventually he was able to open them up one after the other. Kristo was amazed by what he saw. His eyes opened wider, his jaw dropped, he froze.

Kristo did not know how long he stood this way but he slowly regained his consciousness. His jaw closed by itself making quite a loud noise. He then blinked several times, swallowed his saliva and came to himself.

"How beautiful!" He thought.

Kristo began turning his head in every direction very slowly. His eyes were wide open and he looked as if he wasn't breathing. There was such a big variety of colors that Kristo had never seen in his entire life. He thought he was sleeping and having the most amazing dream. The brightest panorama was revealed in front of Kristo's eyes. He couldn't even believe that something so beautiful existed. As he lowered his head, he noticed that something was crawling beside him. Surprised, he quickly lifted his leg but that something disappeared as quickly as it had approached him. At that moment, Kristo did not know yet that it was just one of the small lizards that inhabited this land. A few moments later, something flew around him and grazed his nose on its way. Kristo snorted.

"Hey hey hey! Wait! Tell me who you are!" shouted Kristo. But it was too late. The stranger disappeared in the air.

"What a miracle!" thought Kristo as he lost sight of it.

"Who was that? Hmmm…"

He then began listening attentively to the different kinds of sounds that rang in his ears. He sat down, raised one of his ears and enjoyed the music. So nice it was. He did not know that this melody was performed by all kinds of little birds, grasshoppers, frogs and other inhabitants of this place. He just closed his eyes and listened to nature's music.

All of a sudden, Kristo felt a slap on the back of the head which brought him back to reality. Kristo instantly jumped up.

"Who are you and what are you doing here?" firmly asked the stranger. "You too you came here to make fun of me? I'm sick of everybody that passes by and does that! Tell me right now, otherwise I don't know what I'm going to do with you."

He was going to say something else but Kristo interrupted him. He took a few steps back then proudly raised his head and answered:

"First of all, my name is Kristo."

"Second of all, it is my personal business what I'm doing here."

"Third of all, I did not see a reason to make fun of you and if you want to teach me a lesson that would be wrong. I also know how to deal with strangers."

To prove it, Kristo sharply turned around and with the tip of his tail touched a few dry twigs that lay between the legs of the offender. The twigs instantly burst into flames causing the stranger to panic.

Not expecting such a surprise, Kristo's opponent started jumping from one leg to the other and making funny noises.

"Huh… huh… what is this?! Ouch, stop it or you'll set me on fire!"

It was such a funny moment that Kristo forgot about everything, fell on his back and started laughing. Never had he laughed so hard in his life. By the time Kristo finally regained his breath, the fire was put out. It was the stranger that put it out, not by desire but fear.

"Alright, alright, enough with the laughing," he said with authority. "It is the only thing which makes you all happy isn't it? But it hurts."

He then turned around but did not leave, just carefully took a few steps to the side suspiciously looking at the burned twigs.

Thinking about the stranger's dance around the fire, Kristo got up trying not to laugh again.

"Alright," he said to him with a smile on his face. "I will not laugh anymore. Let's rather talk and be friends."

After hearing those words, the stranger slowly turned around and with self-respect pronounced:

"I'm Groofy. I'm a lonely but very proud bird."

Kristo suddenly noticed that Groofy wasn't looking straight at him but slightly to the side as if somebody was hiding behind him. Kristo sharply turned his head but nobody was there. He then turned back to the dancer (that was Groofy's nickname given by Kristo) and stood right in front of him, staring at his eyes and noticed that he still wasn't looking straight. What's going on?" He asked.

"Stop turning around, no one's there. It's just a squint I have; it's a kind of disease that I have."

Kristo took a closer look and noticed that Groofy's pupils pointed directly to the base of his beak. Another surge of laughter hit him but in order to keep it in, he firmly closed his jaw and squished his paws together. By doing so he managed to control his laugh and he finally breathed out.

"I-I-I-I-I understand," he answered.

Kristo knew that it was not the best thing to say, rather silly, but nothing came to his mind at that moment.

"But how did that happen? How did you get sick?"

Hesitating, Groofy decided to tell his story nevertheless, and it was obvious that he felt uncomfortable.

"It's a short story. Back then I used to live in my country and I wasn't cross-eyed. My friends and I once decided to go pay a visit to another group of friends and as we were flying, a very beautiful bird flew by. So I stared. Then all I remember is hitting something. My vision became dark, I saw little stars and when I regained consciousness, I was laying under a tree. As I then realized, I flew into a baobab. It's a big kind of tree."

For an instance, Kristo imagined this scenario after which his nostrils opened wide and he had to clinch his teeth once again.

"What happened next?" he asked.

"Next... Next, I decided to go back home and bring myself back to normal. After I took off, then I landed but it was not my home."

"Where?" asked Kristo.

"Right here," answered Groofy.

"No way!" exclaimed Kristo.

"As you can see even this is possible."

"I am so sorry for you my friend. Have you not tried to find your way back home?"

"Honestly, I haven't. At first, I missed my home but then got used to this. And after I was just afraid that I would fly in the wrong direction so I then decided to stay. I like it here. It's just that sometimes it gets cold here. But it's alright I'm used to it."

"It's a very sad story," said Kristo with sympathy. "If you ever need help, tell me, we will come up with an idea together."

"Thank you. Now let me ask you a question," said Groofy.

"Yes of course."

"The thing is that I have been living here for a long time and have never met someone like you, especially with a tail like that. Who are you and where do you come from?"

Kristo had no choice but to tell him his story.

After a short reflection, Groofy asked:

"So you are looking for Kretonia?"

"Yes and if you know which way it is, please let me know."

"Unfortunately I have never heard of such a country and don't know where it is. It is because ever since I got here, I have never left this place. But if you descend the valley, then maybe you will meet someone."

"Thank you Groofy, I will leave right away then."

"No, don't go now. The sun is going down and it will be dark soon and that means that your chances of meeting someone are slim. Everybody goes to sleep at this time. Instead let's go to my place overnight and you could continue your journey at sunrise."

Kristo carefully reflected and agreed. Groofy brought him to his nest which is located near the cave as we remember and offered to him something to eat. He gave him a few chest nuts, some dry mushrooms, and an apple but as he saw Kristo was undecided to eat, he said:
"Don't be afraid, just try it."
Kristo carefully took the nut and cracked it open. Chewed it up and with admiration admitted that it was very delicious. After he was done with the nuts he moved onto the mushrooms. As they also left a good taste in his mouth, he took a bite of the apple and Kristo closed his eyes and moaned with pleasure. As he finished his supper, with delight, he concluded: this is unbelievable!
"You some want more?"
"No, no thank you I am already full."
"If you want to drink some water, there is a running brook a few steps away."
"With pleasure," said Kristo as he headed that way.

When he came back, they continued their conversation for not long. Groofy then proposed to sleep and Kristo did not hesitate. He was impatiently waiting for the next day.
Making himself comfortable, he wished his neighbour a good night and closed his eyes.

Kerg arrived home and headed right bed on which he sat and looked down. Kvila noticed it.
"Has something happened my dear? Who was that old Kretonian? I was worrying this whole time. Did something happen to Kristo? Tell me, don't torment me. I don't know what to think."
Kvila's sounded exasperated.
"I will tell you everything, just stop worrying so much. Nothing has happened yet. Go put Kerta to sleep and then come back."

Upset, Kvila wanted to ask something else but decided to do what her husband had suggested. It did not take her long as she was sitting next to Kerg in no time, impatiently looking at him.

"It was the old Kroople. I think you've heard of him."

"Yes, I have of course. Everybody says he is weird."

"He's not weird at all. He's very decent and is the wisest of all the Kretonians that live here. I am very happy that I met him. He opened my eyes to many big things. I greatly regret that we all perceived him in the wrong way."

"So what happened?" anxiously asked Kvila. "What did he tell you? I have never seen you so depressed."

"Please do not worry about me my dear, but get ready to hear me out. I am asking you to be very patient and listen until the end."

Kerg described the content of his conversation with Kroople without forgetting a word. As he finished, he slowly turned his head towards Kvila. She was sitting and staring at the ceiling with a renounced look and large tears running down her face. It is in such a condition that they spent the whole night together until the early morning.

"You think he will come back Kerg?" finally asked Kvila as a new flow of tears appeared.

Kerg was silent for a bit, but with a confident voice then said:

"I believe he will come back."

Kvila was desperately gulping but finally started to calm down after she laid her head on Kerg's shoulder. Talking to herself, she then whispered:

"My son is a hero."

Kerg firmly held her against his chest.

"I am proud of Kristo."

They stayed this way not for long until Kerg reminded her that Kerta was about to wake up as it was soon breakfast time.

Kvila heavily got up and headed towards the kitchen. From where she asked:

"What are we going to do?"

"I want to meet with Kroople again. We will both try to gather everybody together where he will tell everyone who we are and where we are from. Everybody must know. That is the first thing. Secondly, during the gathering we have to decide what our long-term destiny will be. We will then see what we will have to do next."

"I think you're right dear."

Having a hard time opening his eyes, Kristo woke up blinded by the sun. The singing of the birds came from everywhere. The air was filled with the freshest aromas of flowers and herbs. How amazing this is he thought, sticking his face under the rays of the sun. Delighted, Kristo turned to Groofy. He was still sleeping.

"Wake up neighbour! It's about time."

Groofy opened an eye and with a displeased voice replied:

"It's too early."

"Wake up, I have to go."

"Then go," briefly answered Groofy.

"Then I'll see you around," said Kristo as he jumped out of the nest.

"Wait," Kristo heard at that moment.

He quickly turned his head. Groofy was sitting with a malcontent look but this time with his eyes open.

"I am not used to waking up this early, just so you know for next time."

"Forgive me your highness, I didn't know."

"Still laughing? Eat something first before you leave."

"Thank you very much."

Groofy then gave him some wild dried plums and a pear.

"Eat as I need to do some exercise."

As Kristo was taking a bite of his pear, Groofy got up on his legs, spread his wings and flapped a few times. After what he saw, a piece of pear remained in his mouth. He widely opened his eyes and did not move. He had never seen anything like it. Finally swallowing the piece and almost chocking, Kristo asked:

"What is that?"

"These are my wings, with their help I can fly."

"Can you show me how you do it?"

"It's too early and I don't feel like it."

"Please."

"What a beggar you are," mumbled Groofy. "Alright then, only once so don't ask me again."
"I promise."

Groofy took some steps and took off the ground. It was an impressive spectacle.
The second piece he bit off simply fell out of Kristo's mouth. He was shocked by the span of his wings. "They could cover the house under the mountain," thought Kristo.
"What a back! Three of me could fit on it."
He raised his head and enjoyed Groofy's flight.
"How nice and smooth he flies!"
For the first time Kristo was jealous. Suddenly, a voice was heard from where Groofy was hovering around.
"Duck! I'm landing."
Kristo ducked without taking his eyes off him. But it wasn't enough. At the last moment, he was forced to jump quickly aside and losing his balance he rolled down the hill. Kristo managed to stop rolling by getting a hold of one of the bushes that grew around. When he looked up, he saw Groofy sitting at the very same place where he was a few seconds ago. "I'm lucky I'm still alive," he thought.
"So what do you think?" asked Groofy.
"I am amazed my friend," said Kristo as he got up. "It is very impressive."

Groofy arrogantly looked at Kristo and just said:
"Alright, go finish your breakfast. It's time."

Finishing his breakfast, Kristo licked his mouth a few times with satisfaction and then asked:
"Could you show me the path I have to take?"
"That I could. Do you see the forest in the far?" he said as he pointed with his wing. There, you might find someone that knows about your country."

Kristo looked in that direction but did not see any forest. It was way at the left but nevertheless he answered:
"Yes I see it," Kristo replied as he tried not to smile.
He then looked around and said:

"Alright then, I'm off. Thank you very much for everything. I hope we will meet again," said Kristo as he continued his journey.

From the top, where Groofy had remained, Kristo heard:

-"Good luck!"

Kristo was walking through the valley enjoying the sweet aroma of flowers that grew around abundantly. Quite often he would stop and admire some flower which the nature had painted in many different and vibrant colors. On many of them, you could find a butterfly sitting on top adding a little more to the beauty. Every time Kristo tried to touch one of them, she would quickly take off and circle around his head before flying away. He did not mind it but simply enjoyed it. There was always someone that ran or crawled between his legs and every time he would say:

"Oh sorry, excuse me."

He was afraid to step on them. Quite frequently, someone would fly by over his head as his eyes would follow them with delight. He now knew that those were birds. Kristo did not know yet that all the ones that flew by only wanted to take a closer look at him. Everybody wanted to see the stranger.

In that matter he moved along. In some places, the grass was so long that he needed to jump up once in a while in order not to lose the forest out of sight. At a certain moment, at the time he jumped, he thought he had seen some body. He then jumped once more and recognized a gopher just like the one he had seen in the book. Kristo decided to get closer and introduce himself but by the time he got there, no one was to be found.

"I guess we'll meet another time," said Kristo as he moved on.

Kristo finally arrived at the forest. In front of him stood a wall of giant trees that had huge green tops and to be able to see their tips Kristo had to lift his head up high. On every tree, Kristo recognized some of the birds that flew by him in the valley that were sitting between branches. Some of them were sitting and looking at him. He would say:

"Hi friends!" and would move along. Many different kinds of bushes grew between the trees. He noticed on one of them the same nuts which Groofy had offered him.

"I think I should eating something," he thought. So he gathered a couple and sat down to eat them. As he was chewing on one of them, something fell right in front of his nose. Kristo looked up, then on the sides, but did not see anything. He then picked it up, took a closer look, distrustfully smelled it but decided to taste it. From pure pleasure, he emitted a long sound that came from inside. I would love some more, he thought as he licked his mouth. As soon as he thought that, something hit him right in the nose. He quickly jumped up and noticed another of those fruits next to his pile of nuts. At that moment, from one of the trees, a silent laugh could be heard.

"I see, I guess some one is throwing them at me," Kristo said.

With an indifferent look, he sat back to his place and said:

"Can I have some more?"

Not long after, from behind the tree, very slowly looking at Kristo with noticeable interest came out a squirrel. Slowly approaching him, she sat and stared at the stranger.

Without any confusion, Kristo said:

"Hi, what's your name?"

After taking a better look at Kristo, she answered:

"My name is Lidka. I live on this tree. Who are you and where are you going?"

"My name is Kristo and I am going home."

"May I ask you where your home is?" she asked.

Kristo took the time to find a good answer and decided to test her.

"My home is in Kretonia."

All of a sudden, a frightful look appeared on Lidka's face. Noticing it, Kristo asked:

"Has something happened to you?"

Lidka did not find an answer right away but not long after she shook her head and said:

"You are lying to me. I sometimes go there but have never seen anyone like you. Tell me who you are," she demanded.

"I've already told you. I am Kristo and I'm going home to Kretonia."

"You are lying again, now tell me the truth."

"Alright, alright. Just bring me some more of those fruits and tell me what they are called, they are so delicious."

Lidka impatiently put her paws on her waist as she stood there not knowing what to do. However but curiosity took its' place. In a few jumps up the tree, she reached almost the top and disappeared inside it. In a few moments, she returned as fast as she had left holding something in a little basket.

"Here, you can eat as much as you want, they are cherries. Now it's your turn you promised me."

"Alright. Just let me finish them as I have never had any before."

"Fine." she said.

As he finished the last cherry, Kristo licked himself once more and after a short pause began his story.

Finishing it, he raised his head and saw sympathy on Lidka's face.

"Now you understand me, don't you? I must get there and undertake something."

"I understand but how will you accomplish this on your own?

"No doubt it will be hard. That is why I am happy we met. I need your help. I want you to show me the way to Kretonia."

"Of course I will show you the road but you will not make it alone. You need some friends you can count on."

"If you know any I would be happy to meet them."

"They are very hard to find nowadays because Dezmort's rats control the whole country and each one living here is under their suspicion. If anyone makes a wrong step, he will find himself imprisoned. You have no idea how hard it is for them."

"I will then go by myself and think of something on the spot. I really want to see this despot."

"Wait," said Lidka. "I think I might know someone who can help you."

Kristo got excited right away.

"Who is he?!"

"He's a Yorkie and his name is Barny. He lives with his uncle Ralph. I know he hates Dezmort. He sentenced his father to life in prison."

"For what?" impatiently asked Kristo.

"He just wanted to defend his dignity."

"What happened exactly?"

"When the rats burst into his house and began to assault everybody inside, he lost his patience and tried to fight back. Later that day, Dezmort's guards came back and arrested him. You already know the result."

"How cruel that is," said Kristo with hatred. "You must show me where Barny is."

"Sure but you have to stay here."

As soon as Lidka said that, they both felt that from somewhere above, a shadow approached at a high speed. As they lifted their heads, they realized that not much time was left to think as the jumped away as far and as quickly as possible. On that same place where they were sitting a few moments ago, heavily landed Groofy.

"Hi Kristo! How are you? I hope I'm not bothering. It seemed to me that you were not alone."

Kristo looked around but Lidka was nowhere to be found. It iss only when he looked up that he saw her sitting on a branch high above.

"Don't be afraid, come down," he shouted. "It's my friend Groofy that lives at the bottom of the mountain. I will introduce you to him."

Lidka slowly climbed down and sat next to Kristo after which Kristo introduced them to each other.

"Listen my friend, you could have killed us," said Kristo.

"I am so sorry, but I lost my course a little."

"What are you doing here?" asked Kristo.

Groofy looked awefully shy in that moment. Kristo noticed it, so he approached him and said:

"I am listening my friend."

"You see Kristo, when you left I thought I lost the last thing in my life because you were the first one in many years who actually spoke to me. I was honestly very happy that we met so when you left I felt lonely. I then told myself:

Groofy, you lost your first and last friend.

After a short reflection I told myself once more:

"No Groofy, you did not lose him. Go and find him! So here I am. I also want to tell you that if you ever need my help just call me. I will do anything for you."

Lidka stood with her mouth wide open.

"Thank you Groofy; I will really need your help since you know why I'm here. If you are ready to help me right away then I will be very happy."

"I am ready. What would you like me to do?"

"Wait a bit. Lidka and I have to finish our plan in order to get to Kretonia."

Turning to her with shiny eyes he said:

"You see, there are two of us already."

Lidka paused for a few seconds and said:

"Three of us."

Kristo happily jumped to her and gave her a hug.

"Ouch, ouch, let me go before you squish me! Let's finish the plan instead."

Kristo let her go and asked her where they had left off.

"You need to meet with Barny and in order for that to happen he has to come here. You cannot go anywhere looking like this."

"Is it dangerous for him?" asked Kristo.

Very, but I know he is brave and will come for sure. When the sun will set, I will go find him myself. We will come at night. You two stay here and wait."

"Sounds like a plan," said Kristo.

Before sunset they still had some time to talk.

Lidka began.

"Listen Kristo, what kind of tail is that? I have never seen any like it. It's all bright."

Kristo was about to answer but Groofy impatiently interrupted him.

"It doesn't just glow, it also burns. This morning he almost roasted me."

As he looked at both of his feet making sure none of them were burnt. Kristo fell on his back and burst out in laughter.

"See Lidka... he's laughing at me again," said Groofy with annoyance. "He always laughs at me. I am getting used to it. Get up Kristo, show me how you do it," he said as he stepped aside mumbling something to himself.

Kristo slowly got up and picked up a small twig. He stretched his tail and touched the twig, setting it on fire.

"Wow," said Lidka. "This is some kind of miracle!"

"Of course," confirmed Groofy. "This miracle could have roasted me", said Groofy as he stepped even farther.

Kristo and Lidka laughed.

After thinking of something, she widely opened her mouth and shouted:
"Kristo, you possess a very threatening weapon. The rats are very afraid
of fire."
Thinking some more, and with a serious tone she suggested:
"Yes, but you cannot walk around with this kind of tail. They will catch
you and put you in jail right away."
"Don't worry, I will show you something."
Kristo tugged his tail in and as soon the fire was put out.
"Hmmm…" said Lidka, "another miracle!"
"There were a lot of miracles today," said Groofy from afar. "There would
be another miracle if for Dezmort's dinner they served a roasted Groofy,
Veldronian-style."
Lidka and Kristo started laughing again.

Groofy stood proudly mumbling something under his beak as always.

"Why are your ears different?" asked Lidka.

Groofy looked at her and realized what she was talking about.
"Let Kristo answer this time," said Groofy. "I am very curious to hear what
he has to say about them," he said as he finally came closer.
"My friends, unfortunately I don't have an answer. Amongst all Kretonians
that live under the mountain, no one has ever found an answer. It is
believed that something happened to our organisms during the evolution
which resulted in us having such ears and tails."

Silence had set, which soon Groofy interrupted.
"What an interesting story," he bitingly commented.
"That is true! There is no answer to it indeed."
With the tip of his wing, still in disbelief, Groofy waved towards Kristo,
then looked aside but said nothing.
Lidka stood there the whole time and reflected.
"You cannot walk around with such ears; we have to think of
something."
Exactly at that moment the sun had set and the forest became dark.
"It's time for me," said Lidka. "Wait for me here I will be back soon."
In an instance she had disappeared into the darkness.

"What are we going to do?" asked Kristo. "Maybe I should light a fire and it would be a bit livelier."

"No thanks, let's rather wait in the darkness," suggested Groofy.

Barny was lying on his bed under the window. Uncle Ralph walked back and forth, moving something from one place to another. He did this every day.

"Barny, do you mind helping me move these things into the other corner?"

"Uncle Ralph," said Barny without even lifting his head, "we moved those things from that corner yerstaday to the one where they currently are. I am tired of the constant moving."

"We have to do something!"

"I don't want to."

"You are so lazy Barny."

"Mhmm," was heard back.

All of a sudden he thought something was scratching the window. He quickly looked up and jumped to it. It was Lidka.

"Let me in," she whispered.

Barny instantly ran to the door and opened it as Lidka quickly slipped in.

"Hi Barny."

Instead of answer she heard:

"Are you crazy? Don't you know you can't be out at this time of day? The rats can catch you and put you in jail."

"They can try," answered Lidka.

Barny calmed down as he knew that catching her was very difficult.

"So tell me why you are here."

They went into a dark corner and Lidka, whispering, explained to him everything that happened that day.

"So Kristo needs my help?"

"Yes, are you ready?"

"I am, what do I have to do?"

"He wants you to bring him to the city and let him stay in your house for a while."

"It's dangerous but I will try my best."

"Then we should hurry since you have to be back before sunrise. Also, would you have any bandages and some black paint?"

"I do have some bandages but no paint. Maybe you can use some soot, it is also black."

Lidka quickly thought and said:

"Take it."

Barny got a bag full of soot.

"Alright," he whispered, "I have it."

"Then let's go!"

But before getting out, Lidka stopped him.

"What else?" asked Barny.

"You will be moving on one side of the street and I will follow you on the other side by the roofs and before the fortress wall we shall meet.

Barny nodded as they carefully headed out

.

Everything was going as planned. Suddenly Lidka signalled to Barny that somebody was ahead.

Barny stopped and quietly stood. Lidka took a better look and realized it was a squad of twenty rats coming their way. She desperately waved her paws in order to let Barny know he needed to hide. Barny understood the signal but not much time remained.

"Without panic" he told himself. He then remembered seeing a niche in a wall as he was moving along. Very slowly without making any noise, Barny headed back. When he got to the niche, he entered the shelter as silently as possible. He waited as he stood still.

Lidka could see him.

At that moment, the squad moved towards Barny's hiding place. She thought they would pass by without noticing him. But all of a sudden, one of the rats that was walking behind stopped and started suspiciously smelling the air around him.

"Commander!" he shouted. "I think someone's here."

"Where?" he asked as he ran up to him.

"Right there!" as the patroller showed him the way.

Barny sat motionless. He was thinking of jail, a lonely cell, and the rest of his life spent inside.

"No" he thought with determination. That won't happen.

He was ready to jump out and throw himself in a fight against the rats as he suddenly heard Lidka. She was standing on the roof of the house right across Barny's hiding place. With her paws wide spread, she screamed with hatred.

"You miserable dirty rats, what are you doing here? Leave our town alone! We hate you!"

After hearing these words, the rats started hissing as they jumped onto the walls of the house. Each one of them tried to grab onto something and get to the roof. The commander wanted to get there first but in spite of all his efforts, he couldn't make it because of his weight. Lidka wouldn't stop as she aggravated them even more.

"So you fat rat, you cannot get to me... hahaha! As she threw a stick at him which she found on the roof."

The stick hit him on the nose so hard that he fell on his back. Holding his nose, he got up and hysterically started to yell:

"I will catch you! You will spend your life in jail!"

"Then catch me! Look... I'm right here in front of you! Come on you clumsy fat rat!"

He stood on the ground looking up and furiously growled. He then lost his patience and threw a bat at her. She quickly evaded it and caught it.

"Oh! You can't even throw properly," she said while laughing.

All of a sudden, one of the rats appeared on the roof and was ready to jump on her but Lidka saw him right on time. She jumped towards him and hit him right in the teeth. A horrible cry was heard as he fell off the roof and collapsed next to his commander as everybody looked at him. He was still breathing but could not move. At the same time, while the rats were storming the house and were distracted by Lidka's actions, Barny carefully peaked out. He was amazed by what was happening. The rats were crawling all over the walls. Lidka was screaming. Chaos reigned.

"This is probably the best time to escape." Barny thought. "No one is even looking my way," as he crawled to the corner of the next street where he then started to run as fast as he could towards the city wall.

Lidka was well aware and as soon as she saw Barny turn the corner, she threw the bat in the group of rats and yelled:

"So long you dirty miserable creatures!" as she disappeared in the shadows.

The bat hit one of them right in the teeth knocking him out. Out of unexpectedness and pain, he swallowed them and then fell unconscious. While grinding his teeth and cursing, the commander ordered to grab the wounded and head back to their barracks.

As Barny reached the city wall, he took a deep breath and was ready to sit down and wait for Lidka as she jumped off a near tree and landed right in front of him.

"So, let's move on," she said.

Barny stared at Lidka as if hypnotized unable to say a word. She then slapped him on the ear to bring him back to reality. Barny shook his head and came back to himself.

"Are you ready to go?" she asked once more.

"I'm ready but tell me, how I am supposed to climb over this wall?"

"Don't worry, I thought everything through," as she uttered a secret signal.

A mole came out of a bush nearby and walked up to them.

"Hi Lidka!"

"Hi Geery, did you do what I asked you to?"

"Everything is good. The tunnel is big enough for two like him," as he pointed to Barny.

"Perfect! Just don't forget please that as soon as the sun comes up, you must cover the tunnel. We might use it again."

"Don't worry, everything will be done."

"Thank you very much Geery!"

"Always happy to help!"

"Let's move Barny," order Lidka. "I'll meet you on the other side."

Barny also thanked Geery as he dove into the hole.

Kristo and Groofy were sitting and discussing something as suddenly between them appeared Lidka.

"Hello everybody."

Kristo jumped up and asked:

"So, any luck? Will Barny come?"

"He's already here," she answered.

As they saw Barny come out of the darkness. Something was hanging on his side.

Lidka introduced them.

"So, let's not waste any time, you have to be at Barny's house before sunrise," she said. "Kristo, sit down and don't move. Barny, bring the bandages and the soot."

Barny put everything on the ground next to Kristo.

"What is this," he asked?

"I am going to change your look, so don't move," said Lidka. "Barny, could you bring me some water please? There is a brook running behind that bush," as she pointed to the brook.

Barny left to get the water. On his way, he teared off a giant leaf and rolled it into a cone-shape suitable enough to carry the water.

Lidka poured some soot in it, mixed the water and the soot together which resulted in a thick black mixture.

"Perfect," she said. "But what am I going to use to spread it?"

Lidka reflected.

In a few moments, everyone heard:

"I have an idea!"

As she walked up to Groofy and asked him with a sweet voice:

"My dear friend, would you happen to have a small feather for me?"

Groofy was a bit confused but felt like he could not refuse. He then opened one of his wings and said:

"Take any you like my dear".

Lidka finally found the kind she was looking for and pulled very hard. Groofy threw his head back, crossed his feet, and uttered a quiet sound like the one of a mouse.

"Did I hurt you my dear friend?"

"No, no, I'm fine," answered Groofy.

Lidka gave the mixture to Barny and started to wrap Kristo's ear with the bandage trying to form a triangular shape. After each layer she added more mixture. After some time she was finally done. She then took some steps back, took a good look, and remained happy with the result took the rest of the bandage and wrapped his jaw with it.

"Why are you doing this?" he curiously asked.

"If the rats stop you in the city, you will tell them that you have a big toothache and that you want to keep it warm. Understood?"

"Understood."

Kristo admired Lidka. She knew everything, she could foresee everything, and was capable of everything.

"Done," she finally said.

Suddenly, everybody heard a laugh coming from Groofy's direction.
"Why are you laughing?" Kristo asked with a smile. "Do I look ridiculous?"
"Not that much," he answered while still giggling.
Kristo looked at him with a smile and decisively said:
"That's it, it's time!" Kristo said. "Groofy, how can I find you if I need your help?"
"Just lift your tail and spin it. I will always follow you from up top."
"Lidka, are you coming with us?" Kristo asked.
"I am coming with you. I have a place to stay since many of my relatives live in the city."
"Excellent! Let's go then," commanded Kristo.

With Barny, side by side, they headed towards the city. Lidka went her own way. Groofy instantly disappeared into the still night.

When Kristo and Barny got to the tunnel, Lidka and Geery were already waiting for them inside.
"Wait here while I go scout the city," she said.

She said the way was clear when she came back. The only patrolling squad that she saw was far from Barny's house so they could continue on their way.
Kristo and Barny said goodbye to Geery and vanished into the tunnel.
They arrived to Barny's house without any problems.

"Where have you been?" asked uncle Ralph as soon as they came in. "I was worrying. Don't you know about your curfew?"
"I am asking you not to worry, everything is alright."

"Who is that with you?"

"It's my friend, his name is Kristo, he will stay with us for a bit. You don't mind?"

"Of course I don't mind. I am just worrying about you since I promised your father to take care of you."

"Everything will be alright uncle Ralph."

Barny brought Kristo to the table and offered him some water and bread.

"I am sorry Kristo," he said, "but this is the only food we have. We are not allowed to have anything else."

"Don't be sorry, it's more than enough."

"Then let's eat and get some rest."

After supper, Barny offered him his bed.

"Make yourself comfortable here, as I will sleep elsewhere. Good night Kristo," he said as he left.

"Good night Barny."

Kristo rolled from side to side but couldn't fall asleep. He could not imagine that he was in that same city where his ancestors once lived. He imagined them walking down the streets, visiting each other, enjoying life and celebrating holidays with all the Kretonians. Kristo had all kinds of feelings. From one side, he was very happy being here but from the other, he became sad to the fact that his ancestors were exiled from here. All his thoughts were replaced by hate when Dezmort appeared in his imagination with his army of rats. You could hear the gritting of his teeth. It hurt even more when he thought of his parents. A big lonely tear rolled down his cheek. "How are they doing?" Kristo thought. "The old Kroople probably already told them everything." He imagined his mother crying and his father sad and it hurt him even more. Thinking about this all night long, Kristo hasn't even noticed the sunrise.

On the next day, right after work, Kerg headed to Kroople's house. On his way, he would ask passers-by where the old Kroople lived. Many of them did not know but some did and it is with their help that Kerg finally arrived.

Kerg knocked at the door and after some time heard:

"Who is it?"

"It's me Kerg, Mr. Kroople. May I come in?"

"Come in, the door is unlocked."

When Kerg got inside, he saw Kroople sitting at the table. In front of him laid that very same book.

"Sit down Kerg," said Kroople as he pointed at the chair. "You probably want to talk to me."

"Yes, I think it's very important."

"I am listening."

Mr. Kroople, after everything I heard yesterday, I am obviously very sad but after some time I understand that we cannot do anything about. It's destiny. That is why I decided to somehow help in this whole story."

"How exactly?" asked Kroople.

"I think we should get all Kretonians together, in the same day, at the same time, at the central square. At the gathering, you must come forward and tell everyone about our history, everybody must know!"

"I don't think it's a good idea. You know very well that people think I'm weird as they always avoid me. Nobody will believe me. They will just laugh at me and leave."

"They will not leave! I will stand next to you and confirm every word you say. I am sure everybody will listen."

Kroople started to think. Kerg looked at him with determination.

"And how do you plan on gathering everybody together?" finally asked Kroople.

"I will ask my students to do it for me. Tomorrow after school, they will knock at every house inviting them to come to the gathering."

After a short pause, Kroople said:

"Alright I will come and give a speech. Afterwards, whatever happens happens."

"Thank you Mr. Kroople!"

Kroople just nodded back.

"When are you planning on having this gathering?"

"I'm thinking the day after tomorrow since everybody will be on vacation."

"That's a good choice, I agree," said Kroople.

It then became quiet. They were both thinking on their own.

Kerg broke the silence.
"Tell me, is that the book you were talking about?"
"Yes," said Kroople as he lightly pushed the book towards him. "You can take it, and familiarize with it at home. Just please be careful with it."

Kerg picked up the book and without leaving his sight off of it said:
"I will bring it back to you soon."
"No," answered the old Kroople. "This book now belongs to Kristo. He's the only who deserves to keep it."

Kerg stood with a lot of gratefulness towards Kroople and a lot of pride towards his son. Not knowing what to say he barely pronounced:
"Thank you."

Kvila was already home when Kerg got back.
"What is that?" she asked.
"It's the book you have already heard of. Come sit next to me," he suggested.
As they once again spent the whole night together reading carefully every single page.

Barny slowly walked up to Kristo and gently touched him.
"Kristo wake up."
"I am not sleeping," he answered as he opened his eyes.
He quickly jumped up and asked:
"Are we going to the city?"
"No, unfortunately not now, you have to wait for me here until tonight."
"How come?!"
"I am very sorry my friend but I have to go to work. If I don't show up, I will be punished. They will put me in a cage for three days."
"I am sorry I didn't know. Where do you work by the way?"
"In a coal mine as we extract coal for Dezmort."
"It's probably very hard."
"It is indeed. We only have one short break and it's barely enough to grab a piece of bread and a bit of water."

Kristo could not believe what he had just heard.

"Listen to me very carefully," said Barny. "Try to remain quiet. Do not look through the windows because behind this wall lives someone suspicious. Sometimes I think that is one of Dezmort's spies. Every time I see him, I get a feeling of aversion."

Right at that moment, the city bell rang.

"It's time for me to go," said Barny. "You know where the bread and water are. See you tonight," he said as he jumped out of the house.
Uncle Ralph followed him.

Left alone, Kristo decided to grab a snack so he looked around and found a piece of bread. As he approached the bucket of water, he saw his reflection and almost burst out in laughter but suddenly remembering the spy, he forced himself not to. Taking another look at the reflection, he remembered Groofy and understood why he was laughing at him so hard. He had never seen himself look so ridiculous.

When he was done eating, he went in the corner where Barny had slept and stayed there. "I have to fall asleep" he thought. "I have to be in the best shape."

Kristo kept moving around but his sleepless night took over.

When Barny came home from work, he found him asleep in the corner. He had to shake him until he hardly opened his eyes.
"Get up, we have to go soon."

He didn't need to repeat twice as he jumped off the bed. Fully awake, Kristo determinately said:
"Let's go."
"Wait, not now, wait a bit. I have to explain something to you. I think it would be better if you pretended you were mute. If someone asks you anything just point at your bandages and moan as if your teeth really hurt. It might happen that rats will take interest in it. Also, they will for sure ask me who you are so listen carefully. I came up with this idea at work. You are my younger brother, when you were born you became very ill and

until recently couldn't move and have spent all these years in bed. You became mute because of the illness and you can only moan. When I'll be explaining this, just nod your head and moan alright?"

"Excellent idea," exclaimed Kristo.

"Let's go then," said Barny.

As they headed out leaving uncle Ralph alone.

"Where are we going?" asked Kristo.

"Soon, on the central square the trial of a rabbit will take place. It is said that he did not resist and hit an overseer so hard that he knocked out all his teeth."

"So what will happen?" asked Kristo.

"I don't know. One thing I know for sure is that Dezmort will be part of the trial and will choose the sentence himself."

As they moved along, Barny told Kristo about the adventures that happened to him and Lidka. How she fought the whole squad of rats and heavily wounded two of them.

"I am speechless," said Kristo with admiration. "How much of a hero she is! We must unite and destroy Dezmort."

"But how?" asked Barny. "He is immortal."

"My dear friend! You don't know everything about my story yet," he whispered in his years. "If it's possible, I would like to gather all of you together tonight and reveal everything about Dezmort."

Barny picked up his ears but did not say a word.

"By the way Barny, how can we reach Lidka if we need her help?"

"It's very simple, look."

Barny stopped and emitted a strange sound like the clicking of the tongue. He then stopped and waited. Suddenly, the same sound was heard back as Barny looked up and showed Kristo where to look. Lidka was sitting on a roof next to the chimney waving at them.

Kristo was about to scream something but Barny shut his mouth with his paws just in time.

"Remember, you're mute!"

"Sorry my friend I forgot."

Looking at Lidka once again, he simply waved back at her.

Everybody was already at the main square. It was an order. At the very center was a platform that was built high enough so everybody around could see what was going on. On each corner stood a rat wearing an iron helmet and wielding a heavy bat. They did not move. Right across the platform was a building with multiple windows. In the middle of the building was a huge balcony. Under the dome hung the bell of which the strikes were already heard today by Kristo. At the top of the dome, a statue of the Lord was erected which was completely made out of black granite. In his hand was a baton made of pure gold.

Kristo and Barny made their way through and stood next to platform on the opposite side of the castle. They noticed that starting from one of the doors of the castle, all the way to the platform, stood two rows of rats creating a live corridor.

"He will walk through," Barny whispered into Kristo's ear.

Kristo stood still. The only thing that was noticeable was his jaw trembling with anger.

All of a sudden, a strike of the bell was heard as that same door opened. The rabbit came out of it surrounded by rats. His legs were chained up. A heavy stone was tied to his neck. He was moving with a lot of difficulty and it was only before getting onto the platform that the chains were removed. Right away, three of the rats that stood behind him, started pushing him with their bats. With much difficulty and pain, the rabbit finally got up on the platform. The rats then turned him towards the castle and stood behind him in a single line immobile.

Another strike of the bell was heard as Kristo watched the main gate of the castle open out of which came out a rat with his head high and a nose longer than any other. On his head rested a white cap. He was dressed in a long black robe that dragged on the ground. He was escorted by two other rats. The difference between them was that their caps were lower and their dresses were shorter. They all walked with their heads high without noticing anyone. They then got up on the platform and stood on the left of the rabbit.

"That is Dezmort's main persecutor and the other two are his assistants," said Barny.

As he finished his sentence, three strikes of the bell we heard. All the rats fell on their knees and lowered their heads. After some time, Dezmort came out onto the balcony wearing a golden crown and wielding a golden baton. He was wearing a red robe in the middle of which was his symbol, a black heart. He slowly sat in his throne and waved giving the permission to begin the persecution.

Kristo jerked a couple of times. He felt like ripping off his bandages, jumping onto Dezmort and ripping him apart. But a voice inside stopped him.
"Not now Kristo" he heard.. Kristo jerked once more but regained control of himself.
Right after, the main persecutor walked up to the center of the platform and pronounced:
"Oh great Lord, Kretonians salute you!"

A deafening noise was heard; some did it by their own will but the majority did it out of fear.

After some time, Dezmort raised his paw letting them know to be quiet.

After another short pause, with a low arrogant voice he asked:
"Main persecutor, explain to me why all the Kretonians got together today. What would be the reason?"
"The reason that we are all gathered here is because of a crime committed by this rabbit on my right."
"What kind of crime exactly?"
"This ungrateful citizen attacked one of your loyal servants and brutally beat him up. As a result, my Lord, he lost all his teeth."
"Why did you do it rabbit?" Dezmort asked. "Tell us!"

The rabbit slowly raised his head and looked in Dezmort's direction, but did not say a word. Everybody standing near the platform could see his eyes full of hate.

"As you see my Lord, continued the main persecutor, this ungrateful creature doesn't even bother answering to you. That is why I think he deserves the most severe sentence."

"What kind of punishment do you think he deserves?" asked Dezmort.

" My Lord, as a faithful servant of this country and to you, I have found out that this donkey has committed a severe crime. I have decided to lock him up forever but only you my Lord can decide his faith."

As he finished, the main persecutor took a few steps back and stood still with his head down.

Silence had fallen. Everybody waited. Dezmort then majestically stood up and pronounced:

"I have made my decision!"

He shortly paused, and looked at the crowd.

"As of today, the donkey will be imprisoned until the end of his days," he said as he hit the floor with his baton and left.

Right away, the rats ran up to the donkey and started pushing him down the platform. They then chained his legs again and escorted him to the prison.

Kristo and Barny walked back home depressed without saying a word to each other. It is only after entering the house that Kristo turned to Barny and said:

"I don't want to lose anymore of our precious time. We have to get together today and develop a plan to defeat Dezmort. I cannot watch this despot oppress any more of our Kretonians. I am asking you to let Lidka know as soon as possible. She must be here with us."

Barny nodded and jumped out and soon after he was back but this time not alone. Opening the door, he let Lidka in first, after which he blocked it with a heavy box just in case.

"Let's discuss it in that corner," suggested Barny.

Kristo and Lidka followed him. All three looked at each other as they sat down. Kristo began:

"My friends, not long ago, I watched something terrible happen that hurt me a lot. I saw a hero sentenced to prison because he could no longer tolerate humiliation and he rose against the tyrant! He must be an example

to us all! We have to avenge him! We have to destroy Dezmort! To do so, we must unite and come up with a plan."
"But how are you planning on defeating Dezmort?" asked Lidka. "Don't you know he is immortal and that he has a huge blood-thirsty army of rats obey to him? And also, not long ago, he had made an alliance with bats who are as brutal as rats. They are thousands and we are only four. What can we do about it?"

Kristo confidently looked at Lidka and then at Barny.
"We will destroy Dezmort," he said with determination. "Others will then join and we will defeat his army. I will now let you know something."

Kristo revealed the secret about Dezmort's heart.

"As you see, we just need to kill the snakes, take possession of the sword, and get a hold of his heart," he concluded as he looked at his friends.

The whole time, Barny and Lidka listened to him carefully without interrupting him. When Kristo was done, they slowly turned and stared at each other.
Not knowing what to say they turned back to Kristo.
"So how do you feel now? Still in disbelieve?" he asked with a smile.
Barny came back to his senses.
- "I need some water, my throat is parched from what I have just heard."
"Me too," said Lidka.
After satisfying their thirst, they went back to Kristo who was sitting with a smile.
"Yes, but how will we find this place?" asked Barny as he sat back down. "I have no idea where it is."
"I agree with you my friend, that is still an issue. However maybe we should start carefully asking Kretonians, maybe some have heard or know of something."
"I think I may know what you are looking for," they heard.

All three turned their heads and saw Uncle Ralph sitting in the opposite corner. All this time he sat quietly as nobody noticed him.
"What did you say Uncle Ralph?" his nephew asked him.
"I said: I know what you need."

He got up and reached under the long bench situated along the wall, where he spent some time looking for something after finally pulling out a little box. Digging inside the box, with a satisfied look on his face he took out a roll.

"Here, take it," he said as he handed the roll to Barny. "It's a map. It has been kept in our family for many many years but how it got here I have no idea. I have a feeling that the place you are talking about is indicated somewhere on this map."

Barny took the roll and carefully unrolled it. It was a map indeed. Looking up close, all three began to study it. In the top-right corner, they saw a small but detailed image representing the city. Underneath it you could read a big capital letter "K". A dotted line lead from the image all the way to a chain of mountains. Then, from the top-left corner, another dotted line sharply turned downwards and stretched all the way to the point where the mountains ended. At the very end of that line was an arrow pointing towards one of the mountains at the base of which was an image of three snakes. On the left of that mountain was an image of a lake and a strange tree. On the right stood the ruins of an abandoned city.

Kristo jumped up and exclaimed:

"This is exactly what we need! The letter "K" represents Kretonia. The line tells us we have to move along the mountains. The lake and the ruins indicate where the cave is located. It's easy!" He exclaimed again but as soon he thought and scratched his ear. There is one problem though, he finally said.

"What?!"asked Lidka and Barny impatiently.

"I just don't know which way the mountains are."

"That's not a problem," interfered Uncle Ralph once more.

He walked up to the map and pointed to four crossing arrows in the middle of the map. Next to each arrow was a letter.

"This drawing shows us the direction of North, South, East, and West. Look Kristo… this letter "N" leads us North, meaning the mountains are located South of Kretonia. From here as you, the arrow leads all the way down, meaning South."

"Yes but how do I define where North and South are," impatiently asked Kristo.

"It's very simple," said Uncle Ralph with a smile. "When we come out of the house early in the morning, the sun comes up on our right, meaning it comes up on the east."

"That means West is absolutely on the opposite side," interrupted Barny with excitement.

"Meaning Veldronia is located exactly West from where we currently are," exclaimed Lidka.

"That is correct," concluded Uncle Ralph as he left to take care of his own things.

"So?" said Kristo with a happy voice as he looked at his friends.

"We're getting somewhere," excitedly exclaimed Barny.

"Yes but we don't know how far it is," interfered Lidka.

"True, it is pretty far," agreed Kristo.

"The tree you see on the map means it is very hot down there, and it will take many days to get there. I once saw it in that book. But we don't have a choice!"

We have to find that place!

Barny and Lidka looked at him with hope. At this moment, Kristo's brain worked very hard in order to find the right solution for this situation. All of a sudden he exclaimed:

"I know!"

Barny and Lidka leaned forward to listen.

"We have Groofy! He will bring us there! Three of me can fit on his back," he said impatiently as he looked at them.

"Are you suggesting we sit on Groofy's back and leave for this long trip?" unsurely asked Barny after a short pause.

"Yes, since we will save some precious time, don't you think? Also we will be flying high up in the sky."

And then Kristo lifted up his head and dreamingly stared at the ceiling imagining himself flying.

"Alright alright" said Barny as he tapped him on the shoulder. "Come back to earth Kristo, we have to finish our plan."

"Yes, of course, forgive me," he answered. "We cannot lose any more time. I think we should leave after tomorrow. Also Barny, I need you to show me the rest of the city when you come back from work tomorrow, we will go for a walk."

"May I ask who will fly south?" Lidka's voice was heard.

Kristo and Barny looked at each other as Kristo took the responsibility to answer.

"My dear Lidka! I admire your braveness. Barny told me today how you fought the rats and heavily wounded two of them. You are one of those on who we can rely on. It is with someone like you we can defeat Dezmort. But I think you should stay here."

How come? Asked Lidka with an upset and surprised voice.

"I think you should stay here because you have lots of friends in Veldronia and I'm sure you will find someone that will join us eventually. Let this be your task."

Kristo stopped and waited for an answer.

"I agree," finally said Lidka. "I'll try to do my best."

"Then everything is settled. It's getting late, let's call it a night, Barny has to work tomorrow morning."

They all got up and wished each other a good night.

On the next day, coming back home, Barny quickly ate and left to the city with Kristo. They strolled around and the whole time Barny was whispering something to Kristo. But his friend could barely hear anything. He imagined how three-hundred years ago, his ancestors happily walked down these streets. Eventually they got to a certain street where they had to turn a corner and suddenly they bumped head-to-head with a squad of rats.

"Who are you?" strictly asked the commander. "What is your name?"

"My name is Barny. I work at the mine and extract coal for our Lord."

"And who are you?" he asked Kristo. "I have never seen anybody like you in our city, tell me who you are!"

Kristo just emitted a sound and looked at Barny.

"Why are you mooing? I asked you a question!"

"Forgive him commander," interfered Barny. "He's mute. He's my younger brother, and he got sick right after he was born. He has spent many years in bed without moving. It is only not so long ago a miracle happened as he began to walk but remained mute. Since he is able to move now, I decided to show him the city."

All this time, Kristo nodded and mooed.

As Barny finished explaining himself, the commander looked suspiciously at both of them and ordered them to go back home.

At this moment, someone knocked at the door of the chief of secret services.
"Who's there?" He asked unpleasantly.

A guard walked in and announced:
"Chief of secret services, one of your informers is here."
"Let him in."

A pug walked into the room with a hunched back and his arms crossed on his chest.
"Ah it's you! You bring some news?"
"Yes chief."
"Then don't waste my time and tell me!"
"Yes chief," answered the pug as he began. "Last night I was lucky enough to overhear a conversation. The thing is, from the house where I live, I noticed that a few days ago appeared a suspicious stranger so yesterday I decided to keep an eye out. I waited long until he came back home with my young neighbour Barny. After some time, a squirrel joined them. They called her Lidka."

After hearing that name, the chief squinted his eyes and shook his head. He was already getting an idea of who she was.
"Go on…"
"Yes chief. So when they got together, I put my ear to a small hole that I made in the wall and listened."
"So what did you hear?"
"Listen to this," he said as he recounted everything from beginning to end without of course forgetting to mention his neighbour Ralph.
As he finished, he bowed and without lifting his eyes he waited.
"It is a plot," said the chief of secret services. "But we will not let this happen!"
"Call in a squad immediately and send its commander to me."
"Yes chief!" answered the pug as he disappeared.

"What is the stranger's name?" The chief asked the pug.
"They call him Kristo, chief."

At that moment a knock at the door was heard once more as the commander of the squad walked in.
"What will be the orders?"

The chief approached him and ordered:
"This one," he said as he nodded at the pug, "will lead you to a house where you will arrest everyone that is inside and bring them to jail where I'll be waiting for you all."
"Yes chief!" said the commander as he left with the pug.

"We got lucky this time," said Barny as they got away from the rats.
"These brainless creatures didn't even take an interest in the bandages I am wearing," smirked Kristo.
"What are we going to do today?" asked Barny.
"We will finish our last preparations and we will leave early tomorrow morning."
As soon as they stepped in the house, they heard the door being slammed behind them. Kristo and Barny quickly turned around and faced four rats standing behind them with bats ready to jump on them. Kristo slightly squinted his eyes and silently whispered to Barny:
- "Don't panic."

They then looked around to assess the situation and stood shoulder to shoulder. Six other rats stood in front of them including the commander. But they did not show any fear. As soon as they saw Uncle Ralph in the opposite corner their hearts began to ache. He was sitting on one of his boxes all tied up with ropes. A piece of fabric was sticking out of his mouth so that he could not speak. When he looked at Barny and Kristo, they saw desperation in his eyes. For an instance they both lost their heads. They quickly regained their confidence as they began to wait. All of a sudden, the pug came out of the shadows from behind Uncle Ralph. Maliciously smiling, he approached Barny and said:

- "Hello my dear Barny, it is very nice to see you!"
With that same smile he turned to Kristo.
- "Oh you are probably the one they call Kristo, the one that decided to play a dangerous game. But trust me there is nothing you can do. You will now be both chained up and brought to jail where you will spend the rest of your days."
The pug was about to say something else but Kristo interrupted him.
He hit him with all his strength, so hard that he flew and fell unconscious next to Uncle Ralph. With the words "Let's go Barny!" Kristo jumped on the commander and grabbing him, he threw him hard against the wall. The commander slowly slipped down the wall and remained immobile. In his turn, Barny pulled out a chain out of the hands of a rat behind him, swung it around and left two rats on the floor. With another swing he hit another one. In front of him, stood three other rats chattering their teeth. At that moment, one of the rats desperately jumped at Kristo, but quickly turning around he hit him with the tip of his tail right on the nose. The rat emitted and awful cry and ran away towards the bucket of water tightly holding his nose. That one was not a threat anymore. Only five of them remained as they stood one next to another ready to attack again.

Kristo and Barny stood on the opposite side of the rats.

"So, you miserable brainless creatures," shouted Kristo. "Who else is brave enough among you? Come on, who's next?!"

As soon as he said that, two big squealing rats attacked him not knowing who they were dealing with. Kristo caught them in mid-air, smashed their heads one against the other, and threw them away from him.

"Anyone else?" asked Barny.

The remaining rats were also brave though they understood that they were no match against those two as one of them said:
"We surrender!" as all three dropped their bats.
"That is a good choice," happily said Kristo. "Barny, go free your uncle as I take care of these three."
After which he picked up the chains and with them tied up the rats. Freed of his chains.

Uncle Ralph slowly got up, approached and hugged them both, and barely pronounced: "Thank you."
"We have to leave immediately," said Barny. "They can send another squad any time."
"You're right," said Kristo.

Taking a last look behind them, they saw the six motionless rats. One of them remained with its' face in the bucket of water while the other three were tied up. The pug did not count.
Fully satisfied, they closed the door behind them and left.

At that moment, in jail, the chief of secret services was awaiting the detainees. He felt like it was about time for them to come back. Eventually he lost his patience and called for his assistant. "Have the detainees arrived yet?
"No chief," the assistant answered.
"Then send another squad immediately."

He obviously became nervous.

"Yes chief."

The assistant quickly ran out to the prison yard and ordered a squad to follow him.
As soon as they arrived on the site, they saw a horrible picture.
The three that were tied up, were sitting on the floor without lifting their heads. The other six who were unconscious began slowly waking up trying to get back on their feet. The pug was sitting next to a box. He was holding his head and moaning. Next to the bucket of water, stood a rat with a huge bubble on his nose and his whiskers disappeared.
The assistant instantly ran up to the commander of the defeated squad.
"What happened here? Where are the conspirators? Answer immediately!" He ordered .

The commander pulled himself together while still holding his jaw and barely pronounced:

"We were defeated."

"Who defeated you?"

"Those two we came to arrest."

"How is that possible? There were ten of you."

"Before we even realized, seven of us were lying on the floor. They must have tied the other three up and escaped.|

"Where?"

"I don't know. I was also unconscious at that time."

The assistant looked at the commander and ordered:

"Get your squad back together and go back to the barracks. You will explain to the chief what happened later today."

"Yes sir," barely pronounced the commander as he slowly began getting his troopers together.

They could not walk back, as they were dragging themselves.

"What about you, have you seen anything?" The assistant asked the pug.

"Yes, I saw how I got hit. Then, I saw little stars in my eyes. After, I could not see anything."

The assistant grew white with anger, hit the pug on the side, and jumped outside.

When he arrived back to the chief's office, he reported what he saw.

"Whaaat?! What did you say?!" furiously yelled the chief as he stood nose-to-nose with the assistant.

"Are you telling me that those two beat the whole squad? Answer me!"

"Yes sir," after which they disappeared.

"Bring me the commander of that squad immediately!" once again screamed the chief of secret services.

The assistant quickly left the room.

When he came back with the commander of the squad, the chief of secret services walked around the room back and forth thinking about something.

As soon as he noticed he wasn't alone anymore he walked up to the commander.

"Explain to me how ten brave rats were unable to capture two dogs."

"Mr. Chief of secret services," he began, "those two happened to be very quick and strong. In an instant they put down more than half of our squad. The rest could not resist and surrendered."

"What did they look like?"

"One of them was a Yorkie, one of the many that live in the city. They call him Barny. The other one I have never seen before. He seems to be their leader. He possesses great strength. They call him Kristo. But the scariest thing is his tail."

"What do you mean his tail?"

"One of my troopers told me that the tip of his tail burns. When he hit him with that tip, he severely burnt his nose, and burnt off his whiskers."

"You are lying to save yourself," spitefully said the chief.

"It is the whole truth sir," he is still sitting in the barrack without taking his face out of the water.

The chief of secret services stepped back and began walking around the room once again as he pronounced:

"Get out, both of you."

When they left, he walked up to the window and began thinking. After some time he came to the conclusion that the situation in the city was becoming serious and dangerous. It did look like a plot to him indeed.

"I must report to the Lord."

Dezmort sprawled on his throne as the arrival of the chief of secret services was announced.

Without opening his eyes, he gave permission to let him in. Like everybody else, he came in arched, with his head lowered not allowed to look at the Lord.

With a careless wave of his paw, he gave him the permission to speak.

"My Lord, I am begging for your forgiveness as I am disturbing your peace."

As he pronounced these words, the chief of secret services stood still as he waited. But he did not wait for long. With another wave of his paw, Dezmort gave him the permission to continue. The chief of secret services continued:

"My Lord, I came to you to inform you know that a plot against you is being planned."

Dezmort simply smirked as he heard these words and as he slightly opened his eyes he pronounced:

"Go on… this is getting interesting."

The chief of secret services began describing the first incident and how an insolent squirrel wounded two of his faithful solders and how she insulted them.

"Catch her and execute her," interrupted Dezmort.

"Yes my Lord," answered the chief of secret services as he bowed.

After which he continued to explain how one of his secret spies paid him a visit and informed him of an overheard conversation. He then explained how he sent a squad to capture the conspirators and what happened afterwards. When he got to the part where the commander of the fallen squad told him about the burning tail, Dezmort's eyes instantly opened and lightning stroke inside them, but he closed them instantly; leaving only slits.

Soon after, the chief of secret services finished his report and said:

"That is all my Lord."

He then took a few steps back and stood immobile once again. This time he stood quite for so long that his back began to ache.

Finally, in an imperious voice, Dezmort pronounced:

"Bring me the chief commander of bats and to you chief of secret services, I order you to gather a hundred of the most brave soldiers. As soon as the bats locate the conspirators, you will send your troops there. They must capture them and bring them here. I will then execute them."

"Yes my Lord," he answered as he left the room repetitively bowing.

Shortly after, two of the guards escorted the chief commander of the bat army.

"You wished to see me great Dezmort?"

"Yes Vipr, I have a small favour to ask you."

"Anything you desire, great Dezmort."

"I want you to find two fugitives who are preparing a plot. I have a feeling they are hiding in the forests of Veldronia."

"I will send my best scouts, great Dezmort. You will know where they're hiding by tomorrow morning."
Excellent, arrogantly concluded the tyrant. Now go and find them.

Giving a hand to Uncle Ralph, Kristo and Barny finally reached the secret tunnel. Tossing aside the branches that covered the hiding spot, one by one they quickly got in. Kristo was the last one crawling with his tail stretched in case of a pursuit. As soon as they reached the other side, they looked around but did not see anything suspicious so they decided to rest. Uncle Ralph needed much rest as he was still very weak. No one said a word. Only after some time he barely whispered:
"I am feeling better now, I think we can move on."

All together they got up and they followed the familiar path. Walking the last one behind, Kristo constantly kept looking back and soon they reached the tree where lived Lidka. As usual, Barny made the signal and an alarmed Lidka appeared in front of them.
"What happened? I wasn't expecting you before tomorrow morning. And what is Uncle Ralph doing here?"
"Calm down my dear, nothing special happened," said Kristo. "We just taught a good lesson to a bunch of rats."
"What do you mean?" insisted Lidka.
They had no choice but to explain everything that had happened.
After that, all four of them sat down. Two of them were proud of themselves, one of them excited from what she had heard, and the last one shocked from what he saw.
Barny finally broke the silence:
"Listen Lidka, we need a hiding place for Uncle Ralph. He cannot go back to the city. Could you think of something please?"
"Yes, of course, don't worry! I think I know a place where he can hide."
"We have to do it now then."
"Wait for me here, I'll be back soon," she said as she disappeared as quickly as she had appeared.

She did not come back alone; next to her stood a handsome racoon.
"Here, I want you all to meet my old friend Yeny."

Kristo, Barny, and Ralph introduced themselves one after the other.

Yeny walked up to Ralph and said:
"Follow me Uncle Ralph. You will live with me for a while. There is lots of room and I have plenty of food. No one will ever find you in my burrow."
"Thank you very much Yeny. I will never forget that."

At that moment, his nephew came up to him.
"Forgive me for what happened and the trouble I've brought but you have to understand me, I want to see my father free and I want to happily together with him."
"I'm not mad at all, I understand. I only wish you fulfill your plans and I wish that all Kretonians could be happy."
They then hugged as Barny with tears in his eyes watched his uncle leave.

At this time it was already very dark.
Gathering a few branches, Kristo started a fire as everybody sat around it. Still excited about the day's events, feeling like heroes, they laughed at Dezmort's silly soldiers. All of a sudden Lidka jumped up.
"Silence! Somebody is walking on the other side," she said as she pointed in that direction.

Kristo and Barny also jumped up and took a fighting stance.
The noise was getting louder and louder. No one moved. Suddenly, from behind a bush appeared two strangers who stood across from them.
Kristo's jaw dropped. In front of them stood Kliko and Korry. Korry decided to break the tension.
"Look Kliko, it's our friend Kristo."
Kliko walked up to Kristo, slightly pushing him on the shoulder and joyfully said:
"Hey pal! Do you recognize us?"

Still in disbelief, Kristo could barely say anything. Korry then approached him and pushed him on the other shoulder.

"Kristo, wake up! It's Kliko and I, say something."

Kristo slowly sat down and lowering his head he shook it. Finally lifting his head, still confused, he asked:
"What are you guys doing here?"
"We were just taking a walk, seeing how others were doing, maybe trying to make some new friends," said Korry sarcastically.

Kristo was silent. He still could not believe his eyes.

"Enough Korry," said Kliko. "Don't you see Kristo is still in shock, it's not a good time to joke around."
"No, no," finally said Kristo. " You're right."
"Now tell me what you are both doing here and how you found me?"
"Alright, but first how about you introduce us," suggested Kliko.
Kristo turned to Lidka and Barny who stood together still confused.
- "My friends, these are my old friends Kliko and Korry. I grew up with them living under the same mountain."
He then turned to the unexpected visitors and introduced them to Lidka and Barny.
"Let's now all sit down as our intruders will explain to us how they got here."
"When you left," began Kliko, "your father gathered everybody together. No one stayed home as everybody came together. There, on a big rock, so that everyone could see, stood your father with your mother and the old Kroople beside him. Your father then came forward and asked for silence after which he pronounced:
"Kretonians, I appreciate that you all gathered together. Today is a very important day for us. Today, I would like you to hear something about us; about our ancestors and our history. I am asking you to be patient and listen from beginning to end. You will then make your own decision."

Silence had fallen and soon after someone from the crowd shouted:
"Tell us!"
"No," said your father. "I want you to hear it from the wisest Kretonian living amongst us," he said as he turned to the old Kroople.

The old Kroople lingered as he slowly moved forward.

At that moment, a light whispering was heard in the crowd but it soon subsided.

"I know that many of you Kretonians find me strange but today I will try to change your mind. Today is a very important day indeed. Maybe today will determine our future destiny and everything will change. Listen to me Kretonians," loudly he screamed as he began his speech.

"Believe me Kristo," said Kliko, "the whole time he was giving his speech no one said a word. It is only when he was done when out of the crowed a few questions were heard. When he was asked if he had any proof, your father came forward once again."

"Here is the proof, he said as he raised the book high above his head. Here, dear Kretonians. In this book written three-hundred years ago, is proof of everything you have just heard."

"Silence fell again as your mother stepped forward."

"Here is another proof," she said as she laid hand on her chest.

Everybody could see the tears running down her cheeks. Overcoming this pain, she gathered her strength.

"A few days ago, my son Kristo did not come home. He left. He left to the place where our ancestors were born. He left to get us back our land. He left to fight the tyrant. He left to free the others. There is my proof," she said as she slowly stepped aside.

"Your father walked up and hugged her."

"What happened next?" asked Kristo agitated.

"You will not believe what happened next. It became so noisy nobody could hear each other. The young Kretonians were screaming their lungs out about how they must go help Kristo. After the meeting they were everywhere. They even decided to create an army to fight Dezmort."

Kristo sat and could not believe his ears.

"So if you need an army my dear friend, you already have one," said Korry. "Just call them."

Kristo was very proud of his brothers.

"How did it all end?" asked Kristo.

"It took a while before Kretonians left the place as they were all discussing what they had just heard. Every question ended with "What is going to happen next?" and everybody was excited. They called you the hero. It is only by the end of the day that they all left. Your mother and father headed home surrounded by many of their friends, and on their way some stopped to express their respect and say a few pleasant words. Korry and I ran up to the old Kroople offering to accompany him home. All Kretonians admired him and thanked him on his way home. On that day he was the happiest Kretonian.

Kristo carefully listened without interrupting. He then turned to Barny and Lidka. Barny sat pensively looking somewhere else. Lidka was wiping away her tears.

"Oh Lidka, stop crying, everything is fine isn't it? We now have our own army."

"I feel sorry for your mother," she said.

"Don't worry dear, I did not leave her for long," he said as he turned to Kliko and Korry "Now could you please explain how you ended up finding me?"

"Oh that was very simple," joyfully said Korry. "Let Kliko explain, he does it better."

Kliko smiled at his friend and began the story.

"As soon as we accompanied the old Kroople home, we decided not to waste any more time and go out to find you. Korry is right, it wasn't hard at all. You know we have a good nose. We took your scent and headed outside."

"How are the Montronoses?"

"We didn't have any problems with them. We passed by them smiling with our heads up. All this time Korry commented about everything we did. You know how he is. To the first one we met by the river he shouted:

Don't drink too much water you can get a sore throat!

To the second one:

You have such a nice smile my friend!

To the third:

You look fascinating today my dear!

He kept making comments to each one we saw. He did not leave me bored.

When we got to the tunnel, Korry turned to them and shouted:

Please don't be upset my dears, I am not saying goodbye, patiently wait for me!"

Everybody laughed out loud, even Lidka.

"This is how we got here," concluded Kliko. - "I am grateful that you are here my friends," happily exclaimed Kristo.

"What are we supposed to do now?" asked Korry.

First, Kristo explained them the plan they had made; then, the events that had happened during the past few days. And only then he asked:

"So, are you ready to fight my friends?"

"We are," simultaneously said Kliko and Korry.

Barny then interrupted.

"Kristo, I think they should stay here for now. Lidka might need their help, just in case."

"You are right, you fellows will stay here and wait for Barny and I to return," said Kristo looking at Kliko and Korry.

"Alright, we'll be waiting."

All of a sudden, Lidka jumped and looked up.

"Did you see anyone?" whispered Barny.

"No, I just thought I saw someone in the tree."

"Who could it be?"

"I don't know, but I am not liking this. Vipr's bats could show up here at any moment."

Everybody pricked up their ears and listened. After some time, they were convinced that the suspicious sounds disappeared as they continued their conversation.

Kristo then suggested that everyone get some rest.

"There is still some time before sunrise, we should get some rest."

Everybody agreed.

Kristo was the first one to wake up. Silence stood. Tender sun rays made their way through the trees. On every leaf a little drop of dew sparkled like a diamond. Near his nose, a tiny blue flower emitted its marvellous aroma. With great pleasure, Kristo closed his eyes and inhaled. Somewhere near, a little bird started singing her song. "How wonderful that is" he thought to himself, "but it is time to get up, we have to move".

One by one he woke up Kliko, Korry, and Barny. He then shouted to Lidka. Then, they all got together again to say goodbye to each other as suddenly a loud voice was heard:

"Nobody move! In the name of our Lord you are all under arrest, surrender!"

The group of friends looked around them noticing they were circled by many rats. They were coming out of bushes, from behind the trees, from everywhere. On every disgusting muzzle you could see their scary bare teeth. All four jumped on their feet immediately. Lidka was already sitting on a tree hissing with rage.
"Stand back to back!" Commanded Kristo. "They will attack!"

As soon as he said it, each of them got attacked by five rats. A terrible fight erupted. The rats were trying to hit them from all sides. One of them even jumped on Kliko's back and opened its' mouth to take a bite but did not make it. Barny saw it and with a heavy strike knocked the rat off. There were already three rats lying around Kristo motionless. The other two were still trying to catch him by legs. Kliko and Korry had never been in such a situation before as the rats gradually pushed them aside but the friends did not give up as they threw strikes from left and right. However, one of the rats still managed to clutch Kliko's leg though he did not utter a sound. Instead, he swung his tail right in the rat's body. The rat emitted a horrible cry and fell on the floor. Barny grabbed the rats with his teeth and threw them away as far as possible. After that, they did not move. Barny caught the last one with his teeth and with a powerful kick left it on the ground. He was done with his own enemies. Barny looked at Kristo next to which five others were lying.
They then turned around and saw Kliko and Korry both furiously fighting the remaining two rights but finished them off not long after.

"Wow!" Said Korry. "That was exciting! I liked that! When will we continue?"
"Don't worry," said Kristo, "there are plenty of them. There will soon be another attack. And also, don't forget to use your tails as often as possible."
"Yeah I noticed that," said Kliko convinced.

The rats attacked once again but this time ten on each. It was terrifying to look at.
They jumped on their backs trying to hit them with their bats. To defend themselves, they had to help each other by knocking the rats off their

friend's back. Once, when six of them jumped on Kristo, he became very furious and jumped up, turned in mid-air so the rats fell under him, and started crushing them with his legs after he landed. Kristo kept fighting in the middle of motionless bodies.

Lidka was all over the place. She took a bat from an unconscious rat and hit every single one that stood in her way. One of the rats came up from behind and almost bit her leg but she quickly turned around and hit it right in the teeth just in time. The rat flew a few feet away and remained there immobile.

It wasn't easy for anybody. One of the attacking rats managed to scratch Barny's cheek with its' claws making him lose some of his fur. He emitted a loud growl and began throwing punches in all directions. Barny started to push them towards the forest. Barny hit one of the rats so hard that he flew and hit himself against a tree and on its' way down got stuck on a branch and hung there unconscious. Barny kept pushing further into the forest as he suddenly heard Kristo's voice:

"Barny! Come back! Don't go there it might be a trap!"

Barny listened as he fell back to his previous spot barking in the direction of the forest.

Kliko and Korry also fought desperately but got their own share of bruises. Each one of them got hit with a bat a couple of times. Korry was missing a piece of fur on his side.

It is after the fight, they saw the unconscious rat with the fur in his mouth.

Thanks to those two, there was a smell of something burnt in the air. It was Kliko and Korry who took Kristo's advice and used their tails to fight back. The rats had never seen such a scary weapon before and it is only after that they realized it was better to fall back. Almost each one of them got their share of burns.

All of them started to fall back but only the ten biggest ones and most angry ones stayed. They stood one next to the other and raised their bats, but did not attack. Everybody needed a break. Kristo was the first one to use it. Whispering, he ordered the others to take a few steps back. After which they saw him raise his tail high and spin it. He then momentarily jumped back and stood with the rest.

"What happened Kristo?" Korry asked. "What does the spin of the tail mean?"

"You will see."

The rats did not understand either but they did not move. As suddenly the sky darkened. A voice was heard from up high:
"I am landing!"

At this moment, the rats all had a surprised look on their faces. Hearing these words, they looked up and their surprised looks became those of panic and fear. The rats tried to escape but it was too late.
It was Groofy coming to land that blew them right into the tree leaving an unconscious pile of rats.
"Hi Kristo! Did you call me?"
"Yes, you're right on time!"

Groofy looked around him. Rats were all over the place.
"What happened here and why am I always stepping on something unpleasant?"
Groofy frowned and twitched.
"As you see we had some guests but we weren't too welcoming."

Barny, Kliko, and Korry stood as if paralyzed. It was the first time they saw something like it.
"Kliko, do you understand anything?" asked Korry coming back to himself.
"I think that..." Kliko stumbled and continued, "I don't understand anything either."
Barny heard them and said:
"Don't be surprised, this is our friend Groofy, he also helps us."
Kristo then asked everybody to approach him.
"My friends, we have to stick together, the rats can attack us again."
"I don't think so," interrupted Lidka. "I could see them fall back from the top of the tree."
"That can't be possible," said Korry as he started running towards the forest.
    The remainders heard from afar:
"Where are you going? You didn't even say goodbye, that's not nice!"

After waiting for an answer but not getting one, Korry came back and saw everybody holding their stomachs and laughing.

"They're not well raised," Korry added with disappointment as he made everybody laugh again.

Wiping their tears, everybody calmed down.

"My friends, said Kristo solemnly. I congratulate you with our first victory!"

Everybody raised their right paw and emitted a war-cry.

After that, with a serious tone, Barny asked:

"What should we do next?"

"We cannot waste our time," answered Kristo with determination. "You, Groofy, and I are immediately heading south."

He then turned to Kliko, Korry, and Lidka.

"You cannot stay here. The rats can be back in any moment now."

"I will go to my relatives," answered Lidka. "They live not far from here."

Kristo pensively looked at his brothers and asked:

"When you came out of the cave, did you notice a big nest?"

"Yes," answered Kliko.

"Then you will go there and wait for us."

"Understood."

Turning to Groofy, Kristo asked:

"Are you ready?"

"I am."

"Let's wish each other goodbye then."

Everybody saw how awkwardly and how unsteadily Barny got on Groofy's back.

"Don't be afraid," he said, "just hold on tightly!"

Suddenly, Kristo jumped on Groofy's back without any fear and raising his tail high commanded:

"Let's go!"

Groofy opened his wings and after taking a few leaps they took off.

"So long!" was heard by those remaining on the ground.

"So long!" They whispered back as they were slowly fading into the distance.

"Unfortunately, this time, not even our scent will help us in finding them, pointed out Korry."
"You're right," answered Kliko.

"So, I think it's time for us to go as well," suggested Lidka. "I will come see you every day and bring some food, so don't worry."
"Thank you very much," answered Kliko on behalf of both as everybody parted on their own ways.

The chief of secret services proudly walked back and forth along the gates of the city waiting for the squad and the dittanies. Not far from him, stood his assistant and two of his guards, immobile. Suddenly, from where the road turned, the squad came out. He was flabbergasted at what he saw. The bruised commander and his squad were approaching him while dragging their feet on the ground. Not even the whole squad but only the third of it. Almost all of them were crippled. On many, you could see bubbles on their noses, their ears, and their feet. Some of them were missing teeth. The commander of the squad stopped before the chief of secret services and lowered his head. At that moment, another tooth fell out of his mouth and made a ringing sound as it hit a stone on the ground. He gulped.

The chief of secret services just stood with his eyes wide open, heavily breathing, and unable to say a word from all the fury. Gathering his strengths, he finally screamed:
"Where are the rest of the soldiers and where are the prisoners?! Answer me!"
"Mr. Chief of thecret thervitheth, we were defeated! The otherth remain in the foretht, they thtill might come back. The prithonerth dithappeared. That ith all, lisped the commander."

The chief of secret services closed his eyes and said to himself:
"I'm finished!"
He then opened the gates and ordered the squad to move back to the barracks.

As always, Dezmort was sprawled on his throne with his eyes closed. Not far from him, stood Vipr. He too was waiting for the news.

At that moment, a knock at the door was heard and a guard announced the arrival of the chief of secret services.

"Let him in," ordered Dezmort.

He walked in and stood before the throne. He was shaking.

"I salute you my Lord," he said as he stood still.

"What kind of news do you have for me today?" impatiently asked Dezmort.

"Not good my Lord," he barely muttered.

"Why not?"

"The squad I sent to capture the conspirators was defeated and they disappeared once again."

Silence fell. The tyrant was thinking.

He then finally said:

"Chief of secret services, I am giving one last chance. If you don't capture them, I will order to put you in an iron barrel where you will meet your death."

"Thank you, oh Lord. I will find them and throw them at your feet."

"Get out of here," ordered Dezmort and turned to Vipr. "I need you to send someone to find the runaways."

"It will be done. By night, you will know where they hide," he said as he flew out of an open window.

Groofy quickly gained altitude as they smoothly flew above the earth. Kristo enjoyed the indescribable feeling of flying. Everything below him seemed so tiny but so beautiful! Only from above he noticed how many bright and rich colors there were on earth. He could not resist and began singing a joyful Kretonian song.

Barny clutched into Groofy's back and did not move. Occasionally, he would open one of his eyes but immediately close it. Sometimes he thought he was about to throw up, but with his will-power, he managed to keep it in.

"Hey Kristo!" shouted Groofy. "Are you sure we are flying in the right direction?"

"So far so good!" he answered. "Don't worry, if we lose course I will let you know. We are getting closer to the mountains."

Kristo did not have the map but he remembered every little detail on it.

It was getting dark.

"Groofy, you should land! You need to get some rest and so do we!" shouted Kristo.

"Alright!" he answered. "I am landing!"

As they landed, Groofy left a huge cloud of dust behind him.

Kristo jumped off and after taking a look around, he was convinced that this was a good spot. There was a small brook not far. There were bushes all around on which grew berries and there was also a lot of them on the ground.

"Kristo!" he heard Groofy's grumbling voice again. "Please help your friend get off my back; I can't hold him all night long."

Kristo turned around and saw Barny sitting the same way as he was when they took off. His eyes were closed. Kristo walked up to him with a smile and gently touched his shoulder. Barny opened an eye.

"Can I get off?"

"You can get off," laughingly said Kristo.

Barny crawled off and ran off into the bushes. From there you could hear strange sounds. After some time he came back, stretched on the grass, and said:

"How nice it is to walk on the ground!"

"Let's find some food, eat, and go to sleep," suggested Kristo. "Refreshed, we'll continue our journey tomorrow morning."

Everybody agreed.

The chief of secret services ran out of the castle and immediately ordered his assistant to gather ten squads of a hundred rats each.
"We are immediately heading to Veldronia to find the runaways."
"Yes chief."

Shortly after, a thousand rats under the command of the chief of secret services left the city and headed to Veldronia. On their way, they met those same wounded rats who were able to get up after the battle and come back to the city. The defeat was brutal for them. They looked even worse than those who came back before them.

On the border of Veldronia, the chief of secret services stopped his troops and loudly ordered:
"Check every bush, every tree and every suspicious place. Go on!"

The army of rats marched into Veldronia.

Vipr flew back into that same window and sat on the edge.
"Speak," ordered Dezmort.
"My best bats flew over the entire Veldronia, Dezmort. They heard from others that three of them disappeared in the sky and headed towards the mountains on a huge bird.

At that moment, the tyrant's eyes furiously flashed."
"Where did the other three go?"
"We were unfortunately unable to find out; they disappeared."
"Alright Vipr, now leave me alone," he pronounced.

He knew where the first three were going.
"Even if they take possession of my heart, I must stop them someway, somehow," he said to himself. "They must not enter the city."
"Guard!" he shouted after a long reflection. "Tomorrow morning I want to see the chief of secret services and the chief commander of the bats."
"Understood, oh Lord!"

On the next day, both of them stood before Dezmort waiting for his orders.
"Did you find out anything?" he finally asked the chief of secret services.

"Oh Lord! My soldiers searched every bush, every suspicious place, but did not find anyone. We went further hoping to find some traces, but no luck. I then set ambushes all over. If any of the runaways show up, they will be captured, oh Lord."

"You've done some good work, chief of secret services, but I have changed the plan," pronounced Dezmort. "You will bring your squads back to the city and arrange them along the wall. There, you will be waiting the conspirators. They must not enter the city," pronounced Dezmort raising his voice.

"Understood, oh Lord."

"Vipr! You and your army will occupy every tree and as soon as you see them you will attack from above."

"I understand everything, Great Dezmort."

"Then go!"

Kliko and Korry could see from their hideout how an enormous squad of rats was approaching.

"We cannot stay here," said Kliko anxiously, "there are too many of them, they will capture us."

"Let's hide in the cave," suggested Korry.

"Good idea."

Without making any noise and with their tails between their legs, they slowly disappeared into the cave. Inside, Kliko whispered to Korry's ear: "I have a plan! I will stay here and guard the entrance while you go back home and try to gather as many strong Kretonians as you can to bring them here."

"You're a genius Kliko, I'm leaving immediately."

Arriving back to the place where Kretonians had gathered not long ago, Korry did not wait for everybody to wake up and started screaming and calling out those who could gather together once again. Gradually, Kretonia began lighting up. Anxious Kretonians began running towards Korry.

"What happened Korry?!" yelled out one of the young Kretonians out of breath.

"My friends!" shouted Korry, "Kristo needs your help. If you are ready to do this, we will leave immediately to fight Dezmort."

At the very same moment, everybody screamed:
"Let's go! Take us out Korry, we are ready to fight!"
"Then follow me!" called up Korry as he jumped off the rock.

At that moment, a chain of young and strong Kretonians headed towards the forbidden corridor.

Waking up early in the morning, Kristo, Barny and Groofy took a quick bite, drank some water and took off again.

Barny seemed to be getting used to the height and didn't even notice how widely he opened his eyes and began enjoying the flight because of what he saw beneath.   Suddenly, he heard:
"I see them! I see the mountains!" Kristo shouted. "Groofy, right before the mountains turn left!"
"Understood commander!"

Approaching the mountains, Groofy sharply turned which made Barny feel sick again. However, quite quickly he pulled himself together and enjoyed the view of the mountains.

As they were flying, they noticed from afar a lonely bird as big as Groofy. It was a female condor. Groofy noticed her first, and forgetting he had two passengers on his back, he headed towards her. When he finally caught up to her, he gallantly pronounced:
"Good day darling, what a beautiful day to fly isn't it?"
"Good day," she answered. "It is a very beautiful day indeed."
"May I ask you what is your name dear?"

She looked at Groofy with coquetry and said:
"Issilda, and you?"

After a short reflection, Groofy proudly answered:
"My name is Groofyban II Avrikonian!"
"Ohhh," she said.
"Let me ask you please, what are you doing here Groofyban II Avrikonian?"
"I just… took my friends out for a short flight and if you don't mind I will pay you a visit in a few days."

After a short pause, taking another look at Groofy, Issilda answered with coquetry:
"I don't mind…"

She then made a sharp turn and flew away towards the mountains.

"See you soon dear Issilda!" shouted Groofy as he heard the two on his back giggle.
"Why are you two laughing? Can't I meet anyone?"
"Yes, of course Groofy! You were simply irresistible!" shouted Barny.
"And what an honourable name you have! I didn't even know," added Kristo.
"Did you hear how pretty her name is?" responded Groofy.
"Oh yes," answered Kristo, "very pretty."
"That is why I couldn't just introduce myself as "Groofy"."

During the discussion, no one even noticed how suddenly a huge ledge appeared before them sticking out of one of the mountains.
"Watch out Groofy! Loudly screamed Kristo.

If it weren't for him, they would have hit the cliff in an instance, but right in front of it Groofy quickly changed course and flew up vertically. Barny was so scared that he grabbed Groofy by the neck as to not fall. Kristo tried to hold on as well but ended up sliding down Groofy's back but at the last moment managed to grab him by the end of his tail. The winds were so strong that Kristo's and Barny's mouths opened widely as their lips flapped in the wind and their eyes were as big as apples which were hiding the ears behind them. They were screaming! As they reached the top, Groofy gradually gained back his horizontal position and then finally landed. Kristo and Barny fell off Groofy like two statues unable to make a sound.

Groofy walked up to them, looked at them, and slightly pushed their immobile bodies. Convinced that they were unable to move, he looked one way, then the other, and pensively pronounced:
"She must live somewhere nearby, wonderful," he concluded.

He then pushed them both again with his foot:
"Hey heroes, are you going to lie here forever?!"

Eventually Kristo and Barny began to get up. Their eyes gained back their normal size, their mouths were almost closed, but their fur was still sticking out in different directions.
"Ohhh wow…" they both said as they scratched their ears

Kristo then walked up to the edge of the mountain and looked down. When he walked back he turned to Barny and said:
"It's better for you not to look down there."
"I believe you my friend."

"So, am I going to wait for you any longer? It's time to go."
Kristo and Barny quickly sat back on the pilot's back.

"Are you ready?!"
"Ready," they barely muttered.

A few seconds later everybody was gliding in the sky.

Lidka was also busy all this time. Next to the tree where she temporarily moved to, grew a similar one where a hawk and his family lived. He was considered as a leader among his kind. Waiting for the right moment, when he came back with food for his little babies, Lidka appeared right in front of their nest as she was jumping from branch to branch. The hawk curiously looked at her. He wasn't waiting for any guests at that moment.
"Please forgive me Mr. Steerv (that was the name of the master of the nest) that I showed up here without an invitation."
"It's alright," he answered with a soft and kind voice. "You are not disturbing, I already fed my babies so tell me what brings you here."

At that moment, Lidka noticed two little nestlings.

"Awww, they are so cute I cannot help but to admire them! You must be very happy Mr. Steerv."

"Oh yes, I am very happy! They behave very well and you will soon see them in the sky," the father said as he patted them on the head. "I am listening to you dear Lidka. I noticed that you moved to your relatives, did something happen? Maybe I can help you somehow?"

"Fortunately, yes. My friends and I have declared war to Dezmort."

Steerv looked at her with curiosity but did not interrupt her.

"The tyrant declared us as plotters and ordered his rats and bats to catch and execute us. That is why I'm here Mr. Steerv."

"Please explain to me in detail what exactly happened."

"Alright," she said as she explained to him the events of the past few days.

"You are very brave my friends," concluded Steerv after what he had heard. "I am proud to see there are fearless daredevils among us! I will for sure help you. Ten of my best hawks will always be ready to help. Just let me know."

"Thank you so much Mr. Steerv."

"Don't mention it my dear. It is my duty! We all must help each other at any moment!"

Lidka thanked the wise hawk once again and hurried to see Kliko and Korry.

Happy and certain of complete success, she jumped through five branches at a time. She couldn't wait to tell about the meeting with the leader of the hawks and his promise. But arriving to the spot, she found nobody.

"Something happened," she anxiously thought. "And there not here! Maybe Dezmort's rats have captured them?!"

She sat thinking when suddenly a small rock fell next to her, and then she heard:

"Lidka I'm here! It's me Kliko!"

She quickly turned her head and noticed Kliko who was standing at the entrance of the cave.

"Come here," he said.

Lidka instantly appeared next to him.
"Where's Korry?! Did something happen to him?!"
"No, don't worry he's fine. He will be back soon."
"Where did he go?! It's really dangerous right now."
"Where he went isn't dangerous at all, Korry headed home under the mountain to gather an army and he is supposed to be here soon."
"Army?! Did I mishear?!"

At this moment it seemed like she was out of breath because she was so excited.
"Yes, yes, an army! They're on their way!"
"Excellent! We will have a whole army! But now it's my turn to brag!"
"So what is it?! Tell me!"
"I just met the leader of the hawks and he promised that ten of his best warriors will join us."

Kliko was looking at her with a lack of understanding.

"Why are you looking at me Kliko? Don't you know who I'm talking about?"
"Hmmm… no. I don't know who those hawks are."
"Ahhh!" said Lidka as she looked at her friend. "They are very strong and fearless birds. You will have a chance to see them in battle. I can tell you many things about them but for now I will only tell you one thing; we will put an end to those bats!"
"Then we're alright!" exclaimed Kliko as he firmly hugged Lidka and together they jumped for joy.

Kristo, Barny and Groofy made another stop on their way. The night was falling and after a long flight, Groofy needed to rest. At sunrise, they were already in the blue sky warmed by the bright and tender morning sun.

That is how they flew all day long without any stops. The sun was setting, covering the mountains with its' bright red evening veil. A light breeze blew from the east and the friends were ready to land when suddenly, Barny who was sitting in front, slightly stood up and squinted his eyes to carefully look afar.

"I see a lake!" he finally shouted.

Kristo looked in the same direction.

"You're right Barny! Groofy, fly to the lake and try to land on the shore."

"Understood commander!" answered Groofy as he sharply changed his course towards the land.

They were not expecting the enormous flat rocks on the shore to be very smooth and very slippery because of moisture. When Groofy decided to break, he simply couldn't do it. At full speed, like on ice during winter, they slid on the rock and while screaming out loud they fell into the water. Coming up to the surface, Kristo and Barny spat out the water and stared at each other with their eyes wide open. Wiping the water off his face with his paw, Kristo finally said:

"Now that is a landing!"

Barny joyfully laughed and hit the surface of the water with his paws.

"We will never forget this!" he exclaimed with joy. "But where is our best pilot?!"

They looked around and saw Groofy with a pitiful look sitting on the shore shamefully looking down. He looked like a giant wet chicken.

Right in the water, Kristo and Barny burst into laughter.

Pilot Groofy looked at them with a cool look, waited until they calmed down, and then commanded:

"Hey you, funny guys! Get out of the water already!"

"No!" they both shouted. "You come here instead and see how nice it is here!"

"No, that's enough for me. Thank you," he said as he turned his head away.

They swam some more enjoying the crystal clear water, after which they got back to the shore and laid down not far from Groofy on the sand as they got warmed up by the sun.

"What bliss," drawled Kristo.

"I cannot put it into words," agreed Barny.

In this manner they laid quietly for a while, enjoying the warm evening breeze, the beauty of the burgundy sunset, and the clear sky-blue lake. As suddenly this wonderful kingdom of beauty and tranquility was disturbed by Groofy's voice:

"Hey you two! Enough lying around, I think we're being observed!"

"Where?!" swiftly jumping up asked Kristo and Barny.

"If my vision doesn't fail me, there is someone behind that odd tree," he said as he pointed at the cactus.

Kristo and Barny quickly turned in that direction and saw someone indeed. Someone they had never seen before.

"Let's go see him," whispered Kristo, "find out who he is and what he is doing here."

"Let's go!"

Half way there, the stranger suddenly opened his mouth and bared his monstrous teeth.

"Oh! He doesn't seem very welcoming," said Barny.

"It's alright," answered Kristo, "I've seen worse. Let's get closer anyways."

But as soon as they made a few more steps, the stranger quickly stood up and began roaring with anger.

The two friends stopped and sat across from him.

Kristo always distinguished himself by the fact that he was able to deal with any hard situation. This time was no exception. He boldly looked straight at him and said:

"Listen my friend, we too have teeth, we too can fight, and we too are not afraid of anyone. Tell us your name instead."

You could tell that those words affected the stranger. First, he closed his mouth and then calmly sat down.

"And who are you?" he questioned instead of answering.

"I'm Kristo. That is Barny. The one you see on the shore is Groofy."

"What are you doing here?" the stranger asked in a demanding voice.

"Before I answer your question, I would like to know your name. I find it a bit odd to talk to someone not knowing their name."

"Tlak!" he answered after a short reflection. "My name is Tlak! Now answer my question, what are you doing on my land?"

"Forgive us Tlak that we ended up here, but believe me when I say we don't mean any harm to anyone. We are here because of some unfinished business. Let's rather be friends. Come sit next to us and I'll explain to you what brought us here."

After what he heard, Tlak calmed down and sat down with the guests.

- "The thing is that somewhere nearby at the base of a mountain, is located a cave."

No one even noticed how Tlak picked up his ears.

"We have to get inside and take back something very important. We also know that it is guarded by three snakes. So, if you ever heard or saw where it's located then tell us please. We will take what's inside, quickly leave, and be very thankful for your help!"

Barny and Groofy nodded, confirming Kristo's words.

Tlak looked at each one of them and then said:

"You are crazy! Of course I know that cave and where it's located. But do you know what kind of snakes guard the entrance?" he asked as he looked at them once again. "They are the biggest, most merciless rattle snakes that have ever lived here. You don't stand a chance against them. If any of you make the wrong step, you will be defeated immediately. Even we opossums, who often battle snakes, try to keep our distance from that place. That's why I want to give you advice; go back home and forget about this place."

After carefully listening to Tlak, all three reflected on their own.

As always, their leader broke the silence:
"Thank you very much for the advice and the warning Tlak, but we will not go back home until we get what we came for."
"We will not go back!" confirmed Barny.
We will not go back! Confirmed Groofy.
"I just wanted to help, but if you're so decided to go through with this then I cannot do anything," said Tlak as he sighed. "But, when are you going there?" he asked after a short pause.
"Tomorrow morning," answered Kristo.
"Then let's go to my place, you can eat and rest there. I live in the ruins of an old city and it is not far from here."
"Thank you friend," answered Kristo as he laid his paw on Tlak's shoulder.

It was already dark and cool as the whole group got up and followed Tlak. He lived alone in a room of an abandoned house. There was obviously no roof, through which space you could see the bright moon shining and the dark blue sky covered in millions of bright stars. Occasionally, you could see a shooting star fly by leaving behind it a bright trace. The mountains gained back their clear contours. The splashing of the fish was heard coming from the lake. Harmony took possession of this place.

Waking up in the morning, Kristo looked up and saw Groofy sitting on one of the walls with the blue sky in the background. It seemed like he was still asleep, but it wasn't so. He was like a night guard, observing everything from up top, and protecting the sleep of his friends. Groofy saw how Kristo slightly moved and opened his eyes. With a light wave of his wing, he greeted his best friend.

Groofy felt towards Kristo the most indescribable brotherly love. To lose his friend would be the scariest thing for him. He swore to himself that the first one who does any harm to Kristo, he will grab him, lift him high in the sky, and drop him in the deepest gorge.

Kristo looked in the direction where Barny slept, and saw him laying on the ground looking back at him. Kristo understood that he did not sleep all night long and it made him feel sad because he understood that his loyal friends would risk their lives on this day for his sake.

"For them, I will give my own life if I have to," he thought.

After which he looked up again and waved to Groofy to join them.

When they got together, Tlak walked up to them and stood beside them.

"So my friend," said Kristo as he turned to him. "Thank you very much for your hospitality, but we have to go. Let's bid each other goodbye."

Kristo made a step towards Tlak to hug him but surprisingly he stepped back and said:

"I am not saying goodbye, I am coming with you!"

Everybody looked at each other, no one expected that, and all of a sudden… "I am coming with you".

"Did we mishear?" asked Barny. "Did you say that you were coming with us?"

"Yes, that is exactly what I said."

"But yesterday you dissuaded us to go to the cave," joined Kristo.

"Yes, that was yesterday. However, I changed my mind overnight and decided to join you."

As suddenly everybody heard Groofy's laugh.

"Why are you laughing pal?" asked Kristo surprised.

"He too has become crazy overnight just like us, isn't that funny!"

After some time, the rest of them finally understood what Groofy meant and all together they burst into laughter after which they threw themselves on Tlak to hug him.

"Thank you my friend," each one of them pronounced.

Accepting everybody's gratitude, and thanking them in return, with a calm and firm tone he said:

Before we go there, I need to give you all some instructions.

They all sat down, and with strained attention began to listen.

Remember my friends, began Tlak. They closer we will get to the cave, the more careful we will have to be. We have to pay attention where we step. The snake may appear where you least expect it. It can hide in the sand and attack from there. You have to be ready for it and immediately jump away as far as you can. Don't let it get close to you. You have to keep your distances and be ready to manoeuvre. Just one strike might be the last one for any of you. You have to instantly attack when she retreats after her strike. After each hit, you have to quickly jump back and wait for another convenient opportunity. You must hit her only on the head and always keep an eye on her tail. The snake may hit with devastating force leaving no chance to survive. If at some point anyone of you think you defeat the snake, you are wrong. It's just playing dead and waiting for another chance to strike. So you have to go around her, jump on top of her head squeezing it, and only then stick your teeth.

Everybody listened to Tlak trying to retain every detail that was said.

" I think that is it, he finally said. I will go first. Groofy, you will need to find a ledge on a cliff and from there observe the situation. We might need your help at any moment so you will have to be ready, said Tlak.
" I will be ready!" Confidently answered Groofy.
"Then let's go!" Said Kristo with determination.
" Let's go!" Added Barny.

Groofy flew up not too high. He circled around the three that remained on the ground. Tlak was in the front, Kristo followed, and Barny was last.

The cave was situated not far from where Tlak lived and in a short amount of time they walked more than half of the distance when suddenly Tlak stopped.
" From now on, we have to move very carefully. We have to watch our every step and be on alert."

They moved forward and not long after Tlak stopped again. He raised his paw and pointed in the direction of the mountain.
"What's there?" asked Kristo.
"Look carefully at the black spot at the base of the mountain."

Kristo took a good look and saw a big hole between two ledges. If it wasn't for Tlak, Kristo would have been already standing at the entrance of the cave. He heard the gritting of Kristo's teeth and saw how ready he was to jump inside. At the very same moment, barring the way Tlak said: "Kristo! Don't be silly. Stay cool! You cannot fight the snakes in this condition. You will die and leave your friends in trouble if so."

"You're right," calmly answered Kristo. "Forgive me."

"Let's keep moving," calmly commanded Tlak.

Suddenly, a huge fountain of sand raised before them and a rattle snake flew out at the speed of lightning. Widely opening its' mouth and revealing two monstrous fangs, it attacked Tlak. However, as he was ready for this threat, he evaded it and jumped away. Missing its' attack, the snake pulled back and threateningly began hissing and rattling the tip of its tail. It was preparing for another attack.

Without leaving the snake out of sight, Tlak ordered Kristo and Barny to stay close to each other and keep moving.

"I will take care of this one!" he shouted.

Kristo and Barny walked on the hot sand barely touching it. It seemed like they were walking on air. Neither of them looked back understanding that any wrong little move could become their last. They didn't look at each other as well. Step by step they approached the entrance of the cave and stood still. The two friends understood that the remaining two snakes were inside the cave.

"Let's go further, they're there," whispered Kristo without turning his head.

But as soon as they made the first step, a five foot long snake crawled out of the cave also hissing and rattling its' tail.

Without blinking, it slowly began approaching towards Barny.

"Kristo!" he whispered. "She obviously picked me, so as soon as we'll begin fighting, try to get inside the cave. Don't worry about me; I will try to deal with her myself."

"Alright, but be careful!" Kristo answered back.

"Good luck to you too."

Tlak seized the right moment without leaving the snake out of sight. He then made a careful step forward trying to provoke an attack. He got lucky. The snake attacked once again but missed. At this moment, Tlak jumped back and exposed his teeth.

"Come on, try again you nasty creature!" he told her. "Come on, I'm right here!"

Tlak's behaviour and his words made the snake even madder. With short and quick movements, the snake advanced. Tlak always evaded them. But once, she managed to sting him in the leg. Tlak screamed in pain but by reflex he stuck his teeth just below her head. Momentarily, she let go of his leg and crawled back. After which she rolled up and began hissing with anger. She was hurt at this moment also. A few red drops appeared on her body but she was ready to attack again.

Tlak felt like he was getting weaker. His head began to spin and his bitten leg began to hurt him. He then limped aside and slowly lowered his head. The snake noticed it and after a short pause made a desperate strike. But she was wrong because during the time while she was getting ready for another attack, Tlak came back to himself.

When it seemed that the snake's fangs were going to penetrate Tlak's body, with a sharp movement he turned around and grabbed her with his teeth by the head. The snake winded and hit against the ground but Tlak held her tight. He strongly shook his head side to side and felt that the snake did not move anymore. He then threw her away from him and waited. She wasn't moving but her jaw was still wide open. Only her eyes closed. Knowing she might be just playing dead, Tlak carefully walked around her and stood behind her. He waited a few moments then suddenly jumped on top of her and started to bite her all over the body. Convinced that the snake was dead he emitted a long victory war-cry.

Barny tensed as he waited for the snake's attack. It was approaching him with confidence. The distance between them was decreasing and at one moment the snake jumped aiming for Barny's head. By reflex, he took a few steps back, quickly stood on his rear paws, and with his front ones grabbed her by the head. Their eyes met. Barny had a deadly grip onto her trying to squeeze as hard as possible. The snake's enormous jaw was right in front of his muzzle but he was holding it tight. He knew he could not let her go. Unable to find an opportunity to get free she began to twitch and wind and one of her movements managed to throw them on the ground. Barny fell on his back but did not let go of her. The snake then heavily swung at him with its' tail but even that did not help. In return, Barny replied with a strike of his rear paw and with his claw, ripped her skin on the stomach. The snake twitched from pain but continued to fight. She winded around Barny a few times and began to squeeze him. Not to get crushed, Barny had to strain his muscles. But the snake was squeezing him harder and harder. For an instance, it seemed like it was getting dark in his eyes and the grip was weakening him. Only then he hoarsely shouted: "Grooofyyy! Heeelp meee!"

He did not need to wait for Groofy as he saw everything from above and was ready to throw himself at any moment. As soon as he heard his name, he immediately flew down and began to attack the snake with his beak. With one if his hits, he got her right in the head. It was a deadly strike. The snake's jaw slowly closed followed by her eyes. Her rings slowly began to loosen up which helped Barny, who was deprived of strength, to get free. He was still holding the head not realizing the snake was finished. Seeing that, Groofy went up to help him once again.
"Give me this big worm," he said. "It does not live here anymore, I'll move it to another place."

He grabbed her by the head, flew up very high, and dumped her somewhere in the mountains.

Carefully looking in front of him, Kristo sneaked into the cave. He looked around but did not see anyone. It is only when he looked afar that he saw a marble table and on top of it a crystal chest. Under the table, a sword of an amazing beauty hung on two golden chains. Forgetting about the danger, he began running towards the table but suddenly stopped. A rattle snake crawled out from behind the table. It was even bigger than the ones he saw before. She quietly settled down in front of the table, pulled in her head, and turned her eyes to Kristo. He didn't lose his cool and to the snake's surprise he kept moving forward without expressing any fear. By unexpectedness, the snake crawled back just a bit but was ready to fight. Like the others she began to wind and hiss but Kristo did not stop. Then suddenly the snake turned around and disappeared behind the table. It was now his turn to be surprised as he did not expect such a move.

"Something's not right here," he thought. "I have to be very careful especially now," he thought as he silently followed her.

Kristo walked around the table expecting to see her but she was nowhere to be found. Very slowly he began turning on himself waiting for a strike from any direction but it was as if the snake had disappeared. "I know that you're here," whispered Kristo. "Come out."

And as soon as he said that he felt a heavy hit which made him fly to one of the rocks. He then quickly got up, took a battle stance, and waited. But another hit swept him off his feet. This time he got back up and furiously growling he swivelled his tail in the air trying to anticipating another attack. The snake disappeared once again.
"Where is she?" he thought as he looked around.
As suddenly an idea came to him.

Kristo went back to the center of the cave and began moving towards the table. As he was about to touch the crystal chest, he saw in the corner of his eye the snake flying towards him with its jaws wide open. Kristo instantly pressed himself to the ground but at the same moment felt a pain in his shoulder. The snake managed to wound him with one of its fangs.

As she landed on the stony ground she immediately turned around and prepared for another attack

This time, Kristo decided not to wait. With one jump he found himself in front of the snake. He turned around and hit her with the tip of his tail which brought out a menacing hiss. Not giving her the time to recover, he hit her once again. Receiving two major burns, the snake went mad and went over to the offensive. She threw herself on her enemy so fast that if it was someone other than Kristo he would have not stood a chance. But Kristo had good reactions as he evaded the strikes every time. The snake seemed to have gotten tired and suddenly stopped. Kristo used that to his advantage. He jumped to the wall and stood against it preparing to stop another attack. He then slowly took off his medallion and waited.

It appeared as if the snake regained her strengths. She started to menacingly hiss and wind once again. At one moment she retracted herself and threw a desperate strike, but it was her last one. Kristo spun his medallion above his head and threw it at the same moment as the snake flew half of the distance already. The spin of his medallion simply cut the snake's head off.

The snake fell before Kristo's feet. Pushing it away from him, he walked up to the medallion, picked it up, kissed it, and put it back around his neck. He then looked around making sure there were no more surprises, and walked up to the table. First, he took the sword very carefully. After holding it, he kissed it, and then attached it onto his back. Only the crystal chest remained in front of him. Kristo cautiously picked it up and took a closer look. He stood that way for a while, carefully examining the chest and thinking about something. He then finally pronounced:
"You're now mine Dezmort! It's the end for you!"

Coming out of the cave, Kristo saw Barny who was still heavily breathing. As always, the funny Groofy stood next to him. Tlak limped as he approached the others. Everybody stared at Kristo who looked at everybody and raised the crystal chest above his head.

"Here!" he pronounced with triumph.

And right away a delightful cheer was heard coming from his friends. Everybody began to hug each other, congratulating themselves with their new victory. When everything settled down, each one began to recount their duels against the snakes. Every episode brought delight to all. There was no limit for joy. After the celebrations, Kristo stepped forward.
"My friends! Today we won a big battle! We have Dezmort's death in our hands! But a bigger victory awaits us! That is why we cannot waste our time and immediately must go back! Our friends are waiting for us! The entire Kretonia is waiting for us!"
"Let's go!" together shouted Barny and Groofy. "Long live Kretonia!"

Kristo then approached Tlak.
"Thank you my good friend. You helped us a lot! If it wasn't for you, I don't know if we would have made our way back home."
"It was an honour to fight by your side. And you don't need to thank me. I am certain that any of you would have done the same. I also want to wish you luck in defeating your tyrant," he concluded as they embraced each other.

Then Barny and Groofy walked up to Tlak and also warmly said goodbye.

- "I am ready!" shouted Groofy.

Kristo and Barny jumped on his back, waved at Tlak, and took off. In the air, Groofy did a circle of goodbye and headed towards Kretonia.

Kliko was still in the cave eating the nuts Lidka brought him when suddenly he thought he heard something behind his back. He quickly turned around and saw the happy Korry who just entered the cave.
"So?" excitedly asked Kliko. "Did you bring anyone?"
"You will see!" he said as he moved aside. "Come out my friends!" he commanded.

At that moment, before Kliko's eyes, Kretonians walked out of the tunnel and began to fill the cave. He tried to count them but after two-hundred he lost count. Many of them passing by greeted him and soon the whole cave was filled with volunteers. He then stepped forward and addressed everyone:
"My friends! I am convinced that Kristo will be back very soon and together we will head towards the city and take it by storm to get it back to us and to the rest of the Kretonians."

From everywhere enthusiastic voices were heard. Everybody shouted something. It was so loud that even Korry got scared:
"Kretonians!" he shouted as he raised his paw. "I will ask you not to make so much noise because Dezmort's army is not far from here and they can find us at any moment. We have to wait for Kristo and then under his command we will know what to do."
"We understand! We will sit quietly and wait for Kristo," the Kretonians answered.

Kliko then stepped forward.

"Kretonians," he addressed, "Korry and I will go outside and wait there for Kristo. As soon as he will be back we will surprise him."
"Excellent! Great idea! Awesome!" was heard from all over.

Coming outside, Kliko and Korry went back to Groofy's nest where they hid constantly observing the valley

After some time, Korry whispered:
"So far, everything is quiet."

As soon as Kliko was about to say something, they both felt a shadow coming down on them and growing in size. They jumped up, looked up, and at that moment Groofy landed next to them. He almost swept them off their feet.

"Hey guys!" exclaimed Kristo as he got down. "Here we are! He said as everybody began to embrace."

All of them were overwhelmed by the gathering.

"So how is it there?" excitedly asked Kliko and Korry one after the other. "Tell us!"

Sitting across one another, Kristo recounted their adventure in details; about the brave Tlak, the battles against the snakes, and how Groofy had rescued Barny.

Kliko and Korry sat with their mouths wide open not blinking even once.
"What about the heart? Where is it?" impatiently asked Kliko.
"Right here," answered Groofy as he raised his wing.

Kristo walked up to him and took out the crystal chest from somewhere under the feathers.

With a lack of understanding, Kliko and Korry stared at Groofy.

"Don't be so surprised my dear fellows, I can hide each one of you in here."

"Unbelievable!" They both exclaimed.

At the very same moment, Kristo put down the crystal chest right in front of them, and in each one's eyes a spark of hate flashed.

"So this is Dezmort's heart! You are now in our hands!" concluded Kliko as he squinted.

"Listen to me!" asked Kristo. "The time will come when we will have to face Dezmort's army. We are very few..." he said as Kliko interrupted him:

"Not so fast my friend, I have some good news for you."

"What is it?!" Kristo couldn't resist.

"Lidka met with the leader of Hawks and he promised her that ten of his best warriors will join us."

"It is simply amazing! But it won't be enough. They are thousands and we are only a few."

"Not so fast!" said Korry as he finally got his turn.

"What do you mean my friend?"

After that question, Korry got up and shouted:

"Come out my friends!"

Confusingly Kristo looked around. And then he saw, one by one, Kretonians walk out of the cave. He jumped from unexpectedness. He could not believe his eyes, could not say anything, he turned to Kliko who was just standing and smiling. Kristo then looked at Korry:

"Little surprise!" he answered.

Kristo looked around once again (Barny and Groofy also stood in disbelief) after which he ran towards the Kretonians. They kept coming out as Kristo ran up to each one greeting and thanking them. He knew many of them by their name but those of which he didn't he called them "Brother". Kretonians were also as happy to see Kristo as each one of them said something pleasant in return. When the next one came out, Kristo simply froze. He could not believe his eyes once again but with delight he pronounced:

"Master Klinsson! Is it really you?!"

"Yes Kristo, as you can see it is really me. I heard you needed help so I thought: "What do I have to lose? I am lonely. I'll go help Kristo. I still have some energy so I'm here for you if you need me!"

After what he heard, Kristo jumped to master Klinsson and strongly embraced him. Everybody knew him as the strongest Kretonian. Everybody called him "Mighty Klinsson". Holding on tight to master Klinsson, Kristo unintentionally glanced at the entrance of the cave and instantly lost his strengths. Understanding everything, Master Klinsson tapped on his shoulder and stepped aside. Silence fell. Everybody froze. Kerg was standing at the entrance.

"Father!" barely whispered Kristo as he ran to him.

Kerg caught him, embraced him, and only whispered a word: "Son."

They stood this way for a long time without letting go of each other. Kristo finally looked at his father and pronounced:
"Forgive me father!"
"I understand. Everything will be alright."
"But why are you here?"
"It is my duty to be by your side. You are my son!"

Kristo could not even find the words to say anything, he just hugged him even harder.

"How's mother?" Kristo finally asked. "How is she doing?"
"She was very worried when you left but after I explained to her everything she calmed down a little. She is very afraid to never see you again."

These words brought tears to his eyes and pain in his heart but he got over it.
"We will definitely see each other!" he said with determination. "We will destroy Dezmort and then all be together!"
"I believe you son," said Kerg as he heavily sighed.
"Why are you sighing so hard father? Did something happen?"

Kerg stood hesitatingly. He had a hard time to begin but gathering his strengths he looked Kristo right in the eyes and with sad voice he pronounced:
"My dear Kristo! A misfortune happened. A few days after you left, the old Kroople passed away."

Silence had fallen once again.

Kristo let go of his father after what he heard. He stepped aside, sat, and lowered his head. Kerg walked up to him from behind and put his paw on his shoulder.
"You cannot do anything about it son, he was old and his heart stopped. But we all know that he died as the happiest Kretonian who fulfilled his duty until the end. Not long before his death, he gave me his book and said that now it belongs only to you."

Kristo raised his head and interrogatively looked at his father.

"Yes, to you alone," understanding the expression on his face repeated Kerg. "And also, Kroople said he is thankful that he met you and passed on all his knowledge to you, and that you were the first who listened and believed him

Kristo sat, listened, and thought of Kroople.
"If it wasn't for him, I would have never known about the other life on the other side of the mountain, I would have never seen what I am seeing right now, I would have never met new friends, and how unfortunate it is that I will never get to see him again and thank him."

He then sat in complete silence and reflected when suddenly Lidka interrupted him with her arrival.
"Hi Kristo!" joyfully she exclaimed.

This helped Kristo come back to himself and now he was just thinking about his duty and was happy to see her again. He quickly got up and answered to her:
"Hi Lidka! I am happy to see you again! What news do you have?"
"All the best! You will see for yourself, just look up in the sky."

Kristo looked up right away and saw ten hawks gliding in the air. At that moment, Lidka waved with her paw and immediately one of them dove down to earth and flew right by them at a very high speed. He then quickly flew up and disappeared in the sky.
"What do you think?" excitedly she asked. "What do you have to say about this?!"

"I'm speechless! I am convinced that we won't have any problems with Vipr's army. Now look behind you," he suggested to Lidka.

She turned around and saw in front of her hundreds of burning tails like Kristo's.

"My friends," he pronounced in triumph, "this is our comrade. Her name is Lidka. She will be fighting by our side against Dezmort!"

After these words, a friendly cheer was heard. Lidka was amazed! Barny, Kliko, and Korry then walked up to them.
"We have to go," said Barny with determination.

The others just stood waiting for the instructions.

"You are right my friend," answered Kristo. "But before the departure I would like you Kliko and Korry show our brothers how to fight since you already have some experience in this matter. Divide them into small squads. As soon as we get close to the city, they must spread and stand side by side waiting for my command to attack."
"Understood!" each one of them answered as they headed to execute the order.

As soon as the three of them were left alone, Lidka seriously pronounced:
"As soon as we approach the city and the battle starts, I will try to sneak into the city and try to rise the Kretonians to a revolt. I am convinced there will be many daredevils among them after they find out that we have an army ready to destroy Dezmort.
"Very good idea," convincingly answered Kristo.
"I will stay with you," said Barny. "But as soon as we break into the city, I will take a few burning tails and we will head to the prison to free the captives."
"Do what you think is best my friend," answered Kristo.

They were still discussing the details when, after some time, Kliko and Korry came back.
"Everything is ready," they reported. "Kretonians are just waiting for your command."

"Perfect!" answered Kristo.

He then climbed up onto a big rock and commanded:
"Go ahead my brothers! The time has come!"

Dezmort was sprawling in his throne as always. In front of him, still not allowed to raise his head, stood the chief of secret services and at his place, on the edge of the window, sat Vipr. Everybody was waiting for the chief of secret services' assistant. Suddenly during the second half of the day, a knock at the door was heard. A guard came in and notified the assistant's arrival.
"Let him in!" ordered Dezmort.

He didn't walk in but flew into the room and immediately kneeled.

"Speak," demanded Dezmort without even looking at him.
-"Oh Lord! I rushed to report to you that an army is approaching the city and they will soon be behind your walls."
"Which army are you speaking of? For all I know they were only six."
"You are right my Lord, but my scouts told me they saw five or six hundred like conspirator Kristo."
"Only?" said Dezmort with a smirk. "Those miserable five or six hundred want to fight against thousands of my soldiers!?"

He then raised his head and commanded to the chief of secret services:
"I order you to destroy any who approaches the city. Vipr will help you with that, he" said as he turned his head towards the commander of bats who nodded with confirmation.
"Before sunset, you and the chief of secret services must report to me of the total defeat of their army."
"Yes my Lord!" he said as he immediately left the room.
"You have nothing to worry about," confidently pronounced Vipr. "You will obtain what you want!"

"Excellent Vipr, now head over there. Tomorrow we will celebrate our victory! All the captives will be executed."

Vipr spread his wings and flew out the window.

Coming out of the forest, under Kristo's command, the army approached the walls of the city and immediately ran into the enemy. Thousands of rats spread into five rows and they stood along the wall. Seeing the enemy, they began to make hideous noises and hitting their bats against the ground. On the top of the wall were two other rows of rats. In the middle of them all, stood the chief of secret services with a pompous look.

Kristo carefully observed the panorama, turned to Kliko and slightly nodded. He then made the same sign to Korry. And then, at the command, the entire army of burning tails spread out into a single line right in front of Dezmort's army. It happened to be that for each one of them stood five to ten rats.

Kretonians stood with complete determination. Not one of them expressed any fear. They were just waiting for Kristo's command.

Suddenly, an imperious voice was heard from above. It was the chief of secret services:
"Myself, commander of a great army, of our great Lord, order each one of you to immediately surrender! Otherwise, you will be destroyed! All captives remaining alive will be executed tomorrow on the central square. You have time to think before I count to three."

Silence fell. The rats stopped hitting with their bats and no longer uttered a sound.

"One!" arrogantly pronounced the chief of secret services as he looked around and paused… "Two!" He counted as he looked down.

He then waited a bit and as he was about to count to 'Three', a deafening cry was heard coming from Kristo:
"Attack Kretonians!"

And each one, without letting the rats come to their senses, with the words "Death to Dezmort!" dashed towards the enemy and attacked.

The rats were not expecting it. They were convinced they would all surrender after the count of three and all they would have to do is capture them, but they were wrong. In an instance, the first two rows were destroyed. Before retreating, the third row began crushing the ones behind which caused the panic. Many of the rats were left on the ground crushed by their own. If any of them even tried to avoid it, they simply could not.

Kristo was not part of that attack. He stood aside and proudly observed the battle.

"Step back Kretonians!" he suddenly commanded.

As soon as they heard his order, they took back their previous stand. Kristo stepped forward, raised his head, and with a loud and determined voice pronounced:
"My name is Kristo! I came here with my army to liberate Kretonia, to destroy your army of rats, to destroy Dezmort! This is why I order you all to surrender! You will be allowed to leave this land! If you will not surrender, you will be defeated once and for all!"

In response to his demand, a loud and arrogant laugh was heard coming from the chief of secret services.

"You're a total fool if you think we are going to surrender. If there is anyone that will be defeated, it will be you! And if you want proof, then watch!"
As he loudly shouted:
"Vipr!"

And instantly, the bright sun and the clear sky turned black. It seemed that in an instance, the darkest night had fallen. It was the bats who flew off the trees to attack the army of Kretonians. At the same moment, taking advantage of the break between the battles, the rats reorganized and formed up waiting for the right moment to attack.

Kretonians were ready for that. They knew where the black shadow came from.
In a moment they turned around. They stretched their tails towards the rats making one long line of fire which brought fear upon them.

The bats were a few flaps away from reaching the Kretonians. But then something happened which they did not expect at all. From the top, came down the hawks and began to simply destroy them. In flight, with their strong claws, they grabbed two bats at a time and smashed them against one another before finishing them off with their beaks. It was impossible to follow their quickness. In a moment, the black cloud turned into a thick black rain of falling bodies. The few bats that managed to reach the ground were knocked down by the powerful burning tails. The rest, who understood that they did not stand a chance, began flying away in every direction to save themselves. In a very short period of time, Vipr's army ceased to exist. Himself, remained immobile on the ground after Master Klinsson knocked him down.

The rats were ready to attack, but after seeing what had happened to the bats, they began to fall back in fear. However, as soon as they heard the voice from above shouting: "Attack soldiers!" they ran forward by fear and not by braveness. But the attack looked more like a desperation. The lines of rats got all mixed. The commanders tried to reorganize them but it was too late. The burning tails took advantage of this situation and began attacking in return. The panic spread in Dezmort's army. No one knew what to do. Chaos reigned. The situation worsened for them when their comrades began falling off of the wall right onto their heads and it was all because of Lidka. It was she who ran from door to door calling each one to join the liberation army and save the city. And in a short amount of time, she managed to gather an impressive army. She was the one who lead them to the battle, attacking the rats from behind. The inhabitants seized the wall and threw down the rats that tried to escape. Those falling from above like stones, simply squished the ones beneath them. Here and there they formed big grey piles. The chief of secret services fell on one of them. While no one paid attention to him, he seized the occasion to run off into the woods. Since then, he has been nowhere to be found. Panic and fear grew among the rats. They knew they were defeated. Pushing one another, the first line of rats began running away in every direction. Seeing this, many others followed them, leaving their comrades behind.

And suddenly, the voice of one of their commanders was heard:
"Everybody stop!"

After hearing him, everybody stopped. He then stepped forward, threw his bat away and pronounced:
"We surrender!"

After him, one after the other, the rats let down their bats and repeated his words:
"We surrender... we surrender... we surrender."

Then Kristo stepped forward and commanded his Kretonians:
"Step aside my brothers!"

And instantly they created a live corridor. He then turned to the rats and loudly pronounced:
"You are free! Leave and never come back here again!"

It was a pity to watch this army who once was so mighty. With broken legs, burnt muzzles nand missing teeth, they walked through the corridor without making a sound and one after the other they vanished into the forest.

It was said by some witnesses that the rats travelled a very long road before discovering the ruins of an old town that was half-covered in sand where they decided to stay.

Nevertheless, many of them remained lying by the wall of the city. Groans were heard from all over. Hardly getting up and often falling back down, crippled, they did not walk but crawled towards the forest.
"Let them go!" said Kristo. "They still need some time to realize what has happened."

He then turned to his army and loudly commanded:
"Let's go my brothers! Only Dezmort is left in our way!"

The burning tails responded with a joyful cry:
"Let's go Kristo! We will follow you!"

When they finally got to the main gate, they were already opening and on the other side of them waited the happy habitants of the city. In front of them all joyfully stood Lidka. When she saw Kristo, she ran up to him and they hugged each other. Others followed their example. Everybody cheerfully embraced and congratulated each other with the victory as they were overwhelmed by the inexpressible feelings. Groofy was sitting on one of the highest towers waving his wings. Unfortunately he could not be part of the battle. It was not his fault because Kristo gave him a secret order and so he was waiting his turn.

Barny walked up to Kliko and Korry.
"My friends! I need your help!" he said. "I am planning on penetrating the prison and freeing all the detainees. My father has spent a lot of time there and so has many wonderful habitants of the city who are waiting for us!"
"Of course!" answered Kliko. "We will take ten other burning tails and head over there."
"Lead us Barny!" added Korry.
"Thank you very much my friends," answered Barny.

Kerg was the first to approach them.
"I am coming with you!" he said.
"Me too!" they heard a voice behind them which was that of Master Klinsson.

A few other burning tails and habitants of the city then joined them. Saying goodbye to Kristo and Lidka, the newly formed group under Barny's command headed to free the prisoners.

Dezmort was furiously walking back and forth across the room. One of the rats who had managed to escape from the battle, reached the castle and informed the chief of personal security about the total defeat of his army who had no choice but to report this to his Lord.

"How is it possible that my mightiest army was defeated by some conspirators!?" yelled Dezmort. "Where is the chief of secret services?" he asked in anger.

"He escaped without even looking back," answered the chief of personal security staring at the ground.

"Traitor! Miserable cowardly traitor!" screamed Dezmort. "Where was the army of bats!? What was it doing!?"

"The army was destroyed in an instant my Lord. The hawks attacked them by surprise from the sky and delivered a fatal blow. Vipr is also dead."

"How many squads do we have left?"

"Only three. The most loyal ones my Lord!"

"I order them to fight until the end and each one of them will be greatly rewarded if they manage to accomplish this and free the city from the conspirators. How many are they?"

"A hundred," my Lord.

"That's enough," pronounced Dezmort, "now go prepare them for the decisive battle!" screamed the tyrant in anger.

"Yes my Lord."

Running out in the yard, the chief of personal security suddenly stopped as he was shocked. The place where his three best troops were supposed to be was empty. After a short reflection he understood and silently pronounced:

"They escaped."

Standing by himself for not much longer, he looked at Dezmort's window and silently whispered:

"Goodbye Dezmort."

Taking off his uniform and throwing his helmet on the ground, the chief of personal security vanished in the back alleys of the city.

Confident in the total victory, under Kristo's command, the army was getting closer and closer to the castle. After some time, without running

into any resistance, they finally reached it and surrounded it. Together as one they began repeating:
"Death to Dezmort! Dezmort to Dezmort!"

Not expecting to hear something like that, in fury, he ran out on his balcony. Seeing an enormous army at the base of the castle, he quickly ran back inside. Dezmort then bursted into the chamber where the chief of personal security was supposed to be. Not seeing anyone inside, he ran up to the open window facing the yard where his best warriors were supposed to be waiting but no one was there either.
"Cowards! Traitors! Pitiful creatures!" he furiously screamed.

He then turned around and ran out onto the balcony. Bursting back on, he searched for Kristo among the crowd and shouted to him:
"You! The descendant of those who I exiled three-hundred years ago, do you really think you can defeat me!? Do you really think your pitiful cowardly army can succeed!? Fight me and you will see that you are worth absolutely nothing! I am waiting for you! And all of you who gathered here will be very sorry. I will execute each one of you. Haven't you understood after all these years that I am immortal!?"

After these words, Kristo pulled out his sword and dashed towards the wall of the castle. He was not thinking of anything but Dezmort! Grabbing the ledges of the wall, in a couple of jumps, Kristo appeared in front of the balcony looking straight at Dezmort who had his eyes wide open sending his deadly, fire-burning gaze. He was convinced that Kristo would not resist and fall down on the ground. But to his great surprise, Kristo intercepted his gaze and endured its' power. Dezmort tried another attempt but it was again unsuccessful. On the contrary, with complete determination, grabbing one of the columns of the balcony, Kristo jumped over and found himself standing face-to-face with Dezmort.
"I am here tyrant! You wanted to fight me!? I am ready!"

Dezmort stood for sometime trying to comprehend what had just happened. He could not believe that someone was standing in front of him and looking him straight in the eyes just like that. He threw his devastating gaze a few more times at Kristo, but even that remained useless. Then, with a sinister laugh, he instantly turned around and began climbing by grabbing the ledges sticking out of the wall and finally finding himself at the top of his own statue. Sitting on the top of his head, he furiously yelled:

"So what now!? You cannot defeat me! I am immortal! You don't have my heart!"

Kristo dashed to the top and grabbing the same ledges, reached the statue and held on to one of its legs and shouted:

"You are wrong Dezmort! It's above your head! Look!"

At the very same moment, Kristo screamed so loud that even the ones beneath heard him:

"Groofy!!!"

And immediately above Dezmort's head appeared an enormous dark shadow. It was getting bigger by the second! And when Dezmort looked up, he saw a huge bird above his head which made a couple of big flaps, and after one of them, from somewhere under the wing fell out the crystal chest.

It fell right before the eyes of Dezmort who was in shock as he slowly watched it fall down in fear. When the crystal chest reached Kristo, Dezmort closed his eyes. Holding his sword with one of his paws, with a single swing Kristo slashed the chest in half and with it the heart. Thousands of bright fragments of all colors fell like a diamond rain to the feet of those standing beneath.

And what do you think happened at that moment? At that very same moment, Dezmort began to turn into the most ordinary cat. He stuck his tail under and his eyes became ordinary like those of any cat. He emitted typical cat noises. It was a pity to watch.

At the head of his squad, Barny burst into the prison. To their surprise, the main gate was open and you could find the guards' belongings all over the big stony yard. Everything was upside down including the furniture. "They ran," confidently said Kerg. "There is no one here except for the prisoners! Let's penetrate inside."

As soon as they found themselves inside, a deafening noise was heard. It was the prisoners who joyfully shouted and hit against the metal doors with anything they could find as they saw their rescuers.

"We have to find the keys," excitingly said Barny. "They must be kept in a special room!"

One of the prisoners heard them and shouted to Barny that the room was located at the end of the corridor.

Without wasting any time, Barny dashed in that direction. Master Klinsson joined him. Inside the room, they saw the exact same thing as in the yard: total chaos. But they didn't care. They needed the keys. Taking a look around, they did not see anything on the walls. However, by taking a closer look in this damp and dim room, Barny distinguished in one of the corners, a black metal box.
"They're inside," he excitedly told Master Klinsson.

But as they got closer they realized there was a padlock on the box.

"What are we going to do?" said Barny confused. "We now have to find the keys for this lock."
"Don't worry my friend," answered Master Klinsson. "That's not a big problem!"
He looked around and found a bat on the floor left behind by one of the rats. Picking it up and taking a hard swing, Master Klinsson simply cracked the lock in half as it strongly hit the ground and bounced to the wall.
"Now that's a hit!" excitedly said Barny.

Master Klinsson shrugged his shoulders as if it were nothing for him. They then opened the box and saw two big bunches of keys hanging on two small hooks. As the prison was divided into two floors, each bunch had its own floor.

Grabbing them, Barny handed one to Master Klinsson as they ran back to their comrades.

They split themselves into two groups. Barny and his group ran up to the second floor. Opening every cell, they found prisoners crying of joy. With gratefulness, the prisoners embraced their rescuers and ran out to the front yard.

When Barny approached the last door, he did not see anyone next to it. Nobody was screaming there. He slowly opened the door and entered the cell. What he saw inside struck him right in the heart; in the corner, on a pile of damp straw, sat his father. He was not recognizable. Very skinny and aged, he sat and with pitiful eyes looked at Barny trying to smile. "Father!" shouted Barny with tears in his eyes as he ran to him.

He firmly pressed himself against his father and burst into tears. Shir, his father, put his paw on his son's head and gently stroke it.

After some time, in a weak voice, he finally pronounced:
"My son, I always believed the day would come when we would be reunited. And see, it has come. We will never be separated again."
"Never again!" answered Barny. "Let's go father," said Barny as he got up. "I'll help you get out of here."

After Shir got up with difficulty, Barny supported him with his shoulder and helped him walk out to the front yard which was already illuminated by the bronze color of the sunset. Total exaltation reigned the yard. Everybody took off their striped prisoner's cap and the heavy iron numbered collar. They threw it all to their feet.
"Freedom!" They all shouted as they embraced themselves.

Barny, Master Klinsson and Kerg got the most of the hugs. Then altogether they happily marched to the central square.

Arriving there, they witnessed the incredible transformation of the brutal tyrant into a cat.

As much as Kristo was brave, fearless and ready to risk his life, he had a noble heart.

Seeing there was nothing left of the old despot, he put the sword back in its sheath, got down and joined the rest of the habitants.

"Step aside my friends!" called out Kristo.

And before everybody's eyes, a long corridor was formed starting from the castle and ending at the border of Veldronia whose inhabitants also came to see the shameful exile of the former tyrant. You could see those same ten hawks gliding high in the sky.

With fear in his eyes, Dezmort carefully came down avoiding eye-contact with everybody in the crowd. On each of his sides rose two live walls. He slowly began to shake but none made a sound. It was not hate in their eyes. "You get what you deserve" is what you could read on their faces.

Uncertain, Dezmort made his first steps. The further he walked, the more his inner voice told him; "Run! Save yourself before they rip you to pieces!"
His heart furiously beat as he could not resist and without even making it half-way through his path, he dashed, urged by his fear, and disappeared into the woods.

Kristo and Kerg stood across each other in this live corridor. None of them paid attention to Dezmort as he left.

Father was looking at Kristo and was proud that he raised such a true, intelligent and brave son, who risking his life, opened the eyes of all Kretonians to a new world.

Kristo was obviously thinking of something else. He was thinking of how thankful he was towards his father since it was him who raised him, gave him all the knowledge and was always there to support him.
"He came to help me and fought like everybody else! I will always owe it to him!" he thought.

Epilogue

A week has past by since the destruction of Dezmort and a day of celebration was assigned in the city. Each one actively participated in the preparation of this day. The ex-prisoners disassembled the execution deck on the main square. Others then joined them and together they got rid of everything that belonged to Dezmort. Some Kretonians were putting together the tables for the celebration supper as well as stages for the local musicians and actors. For the first time in so many years, the city came to life and resembled a giant ant-hill. Everybody was happy, jokes and laughs were heard all over. A joyous atmosphere reigned the place.

Everybody was impatiently waiting for this day. During this time, our well-known heroes took the opportunity to devote their time to their relatives and friends.

Lidka said goodbye promising to comeback for the holiday and left for Veldronia. She decided to move back to live in her old place.

Flying down from one of the towers and passing by his friends, Groofy shouted:
- "I will be back soon!"

None wondered where he was going. Issilda was waiting for him!

Still supporting his father, Barny headed home. With great joy, uncle Ralph welcomed them. As carefully as he could, he embraced his brother and helped him get in bed. Every day, Barny and uncle Ralph took care of Shir as he got better in time for the holiday.

Kristo also decided not to lose any time and at the head of his army headed to his Underground Kretonia as it was later called. His father walked right next to him. Kliko, Korry, and the rest of the army followed him not far behind.

Walking through the stone valley, at the same place by the river, Kristo saw Juba and ran up to him.
"Hi Juba! He joyfully shouted. How are you!?"

He wasn't expecting to meet anyone but as he recognized Kristo, he stood on his back paws, raised his trunk, and uttered his piercing sound after which he said:
"Hello Kristo! I am happy to see you! To tell you the truth, I didn't think we would meet again."

Touched by such a welcome, Kristo friendly tapped on his belly full of water and with a smile he said:
"We will see each other again."
"Did you find that other world you were talking about?"
"Yes Juba, and it is amazing. I promise, you too will see it someday."
"That would be great!" answered Juba in a deep voice.
"I am sorry my friend, but I have to go now."
"Until next time Kristo! Don't forget about me!"

Kerg stood aside as Kristo knocked at his own door.
"Coming!" he heard his mother's voice as shivers went down his spine.

Kvila put the washed dishes aside and went to open the door. She froze as she opened it. Kristo stood smiling at the door step. With her paws stretched forward, Kvila emitted a voiceless sound and fell in Kristo's embrace. She then burst into tears.
"My son! My dear son! You are back!" she kept repeating as she cried. "I knew you would come back."

Kristo stood without saying a word. He was not able to speak. He was afraid he would too break down in tears if he said a word.

They stood this way for quite a long time.

During this time, from the surrounding houses, came out their neighbours and with sympathy admired this homecoming.

Many of them were crying. Kerg then walked up to his wife and son and helped them walk inside the house.

All this time, Kerta did not ask a question and did not say a word. She just tightly grabbed him by the leg and pressed her head against him

For two days, nobody got out of the house. Kristo told his mother what happened throughout all the time he was away; though, he tried not to mention all the dangerous moments. "I'm not going to make her sad and worried," he thought.

But when it was Kerg's turn, he did not leave out any detail.

Kvila found out about their meeting, the battle against the rats, how Kristo jumped on the statue and destroyed Dezmort, and how it all ended. During this time, Kvila did not take her eyes of her son. Her heart was overwhelmed by the warmest motherly love.

She would smile, then cry, then smile again. Different feelings were felt. But the most important was her love and pride towards her son!

On the third day, Kristo headed to visit Kroople's grave and spent the day there with his head down. He relived in his head every moment he had spent with him; his first and last meeting. It was very painful since Kroople was the first to tell him everything about Kretonians and about their sad history. It was unfortunate that he did not live to see the day he was dreaming of his whole life!

Kristo got up, took off his medallion and put it on Kroople's stone, after which he leaned over and silently whispered:
"Thank you for everything."

On the next day, on the main square of Underground Kretonia, gathered all its' habitants. All of them including families, the youth, even the elderly, decided to come up and take a look at the other amazing world, and take part in the upcoming holiday.

At this moment, Korry took the opportunity to take things in charge. Joyfully, he did not forget to make everybody in the crowd laugh. He had jokes for all, the young and the old.

When everybody finally got together, Korry commanded:
"Follow me!"

The noisy and happy crowd followed him. At the end of the group walked Kristo, Kliko, their parents, the little Kerta and Kliko's little brother Kyde.

The holiday turned to be fantastic. Kretonians were surprised by how much fun they had. They sang, danced and musicians played for them. It then changed into some sort of presentation given by the local actors. The tables were full of different foods and snacks. Nobody forgot about the guests. They were welcomed like the closest brothers and sisters. Everyone made some new friends and shared their impressions of the celebration. It was a holiday of life.

Forgetting everything, Kvila and uncle Ralph went up to dance with everybody else. Shir and Kerg laughed out loud watching them! It was indescribable! Arriving at the party, Groofy and Issilda gathered a couple of little ones on their back, flew up high in the sky, and circled around the central square. Some squealed, some screamed, but all were having a blast.
"More! More!" they asked.

And every time Groofy and Issilda flew up above the city they made the kiddies happy.

Kliko and Korry got lost somewhere in a noisy dancing crowd. Occasionally you could see one of them dancing with a young female..

Kristo, Barny, and Lidka were happy for them as they stood watching not far. However, they were not only happy for them, but for everybody! They were happy for this day that brought them together! They were happy for this holiday! They were happy for life!

What happened after the holiday you might ask? On the next day, all the habitants of Kretonia unanimously proclaimed Kristo as their leader. As the most judgemental, Kliko became his main advisor. Korry began working in one of the theatres and not long after became one of the most popular actors. Barny was named the commander of the Kretonian army. Everybody decided to have one so that the past didn't repeat itself. Lidka returned to Veldronia and after some time she gave birth to two little babies named Kristo and Barny. Groofy and Issilda also settled down to a family life and the world saw a beautiful Groofyssil.

Dezmort's castle was turned into a learning academy, where Kerg tutored mathematics three times a week.

All his family moved to the city where they live together with Kristo.

Many habitants of the Underground Kretonia also moved to the city.
The older ones decided to stay there as they had built a lot underground and it was hard to leave it all behind. Soon after, they built a bridge across the river where lived the Montronoses and began visiting them without forgetting to invite them over.

Everybody was happy and enjoyed every day together! With the exception of one…

On his usual place sat Juba. He was thinking about that other amazing world.

THE END.